White Christmas

A Spicy Novella

RHIANNA BURWELL

Chapter One

Autumn

"They are going to be here in about ten minutes. Can you please set the table?" my mom asks in a huff, the annoyance in her voice making it that much harder to push down my own. I suppress an eye roll, wishing like hell we could just skip our Christmas tradition this year, but I know it's no use. I've been trying for years, and I'm sick of asking, knowing it's not going to get me anywhere, knowing one way or another, *he's* going to show up, in my fucking house, and spend the entire day making my life hell. I walk to grab plates from the cabinet, knowing this is only the start of my misery.

Our moms are best friends and have been since high school. They kept our families close, desperate for us to get along just like they did, and when we were kids, it was fine. He annoyed me, but when you're a kid, it doesn't really matter. I would play with him, even though he always seemed to make fun of my toys and pull my fucking hair, but I was a kid, and I was bored most of the time anyway. Now, as an adult, his constant need to piss me off is just annoying and immature.

Our families have been like family to each other, spending every Christmas together since my grandma died when I was seven. Both of our moms moved away from their childhood homes in California to a small town in Colorado, intent on getting away from the hustle and bustle of the cities, desperate for a change. They moved together, just two girls who wanted to experience the world together, and then they fell in love with two locals but stuck by each other's side the entire time. Their friendship lasted through everything, becoming their entire support system in a city where neither of them had any family.

When my mom was giving birth to me, Carol was the one in the delivery room with my mom, holding her hand while she shot daggers at my dad, not wanting much to do with the man who put her in this position. When Carol was on bed rest for three weeks when she was pregnant with Griffin, the youngest of her kids, the only one still living at home with her, my mom was the one taking care of the rest of her family, intent that she would do the same thing for us if we needed it.

Honestly, their friendship is beautiful. I could only dream of something so amazing, someone to stand by your side through everything, to give them your best and your worst, and have them accept it all. Their friendship is the dream, and I couldn't ask for a better person than Carol in my life, but her son is the bane of my fucking existence.

I don't know when the feud started. It feels like one of those things that has been happening for so fucking long that I don't even know what started it or what straw finally broke the camel's back. I just know it's a constant hate, the kind that you don't ever remember *not* feeling.

Theo is just a fucking dick. He walks through my house like he owns the place, like he's better than me, intent on getting the last word, and constantly trying to put me down. When we were kids, he did the same thing, but I always brushed it off, thinking he was just too immature and that he would eventually grow out of it, but it continued, endlessly, and after a while, I realized we were never going to be best friends like our parents. Instead, we would continually refuse to get along, always creating drama at the family gatherings. Our parents have pushed us together and torn us apart, but nothing seems to suppress the hatred between us. Even though we do our best to hide our annoyance with each other for their sake, it always seems to come out, the both of us making every family gathering awkward, but we can't stop. It almost feels like it's natural, like fighting is a part of us, a piece of us that we can't hold back no matter how much we try.

This year is going to be different, though. I've tried to do a truce, desperate for this petty drama to end, but somehow, it always ends in one of us breaking it, making the other shoot back harder. This year, I'm just fucking ignoring him. I'm not even going to give him the time of day because I'm sick of wasting my time on someone who is such a dick to me for no goddamn reason. This year, I'm not going to let him get under my skin, not going to let him get the best of me. Not this year. I'm determined, desperate even, to have one fucking Christmas, one fucking holiday without the bickering.

It's going to be a goddamn feat. Usually, they are only here for a few hours on Christmas day, just long enough for everyone to get sick of us and get a little tipsy on the eggnog and then leave before we blow the house up. This year, though, his family is coming up on Christmas Eve and spending the night. It's supposed to snow all day tomorrow, and no one wants to drive in it because it's supposed to be nasty. They are sleeping here, which means a lot more time spent together and a lot more misery for me.

That's why, this year, I'm not even going to give him the time of day, not even leaning into our stupid fucking feud. I'm going to be the bigger person because I know for a fact that he never would.

It helps that I know it'll piss him off, too, not being able to get a rise out of me, but we aren't going to talk about that.

Chapter Two

Autumn

The doorbell rings, and I suppress the groan bubbling in my throat, my automatic reaction to knowing he's here. I hold it back, just barely. I need to get myself in the right mindset because as much as I am trying to get through this without a fight, I know the second he is through that door, he's going to do everything he can to piss me off, getting all his little fucking jabs in, desperate to get a fucking rise out of me.

My mom opens the door with a high-pitched scream, excited to see her best friend, and I feel myself smile from the living room, watching them hug, the excitement on their faces obvious, their friendship so fucking beautiful. I adore them, truthfully.

"Oh my god, you look so cute!" my mom exclaims, looking Carol up and down. The red sparkly dress is Carol wearing catches the light overhead, making her look like a flame coming in from the darkness outside.

"Thank you. I knew you would like it," Carol says, her face lighting up at my mom's compliment. She glows under my mom's attention, both coming into their own when they are around each other. She finally shuffles inside, stomping her feet on the porch before stepping through the threshold, doing her best to track in as little snow as possible, and her husband Dave follows behind, pulling my mom into a hug with a small smile on his face, our fathers being drug into this friendship, but having little resistance.

"Oh my god, good to see you too, Dave," my mom says, and Carol walks over to me, her brown hair glowing under the light, looking at me like she does every time she sees me as if I've grown another head and can't believe how different I look, even though she was at the house less than a few months ago. She always does this, in a constant state of shock at how much I've grown, how the time flies. It would be annoying if Carol weren't like an aunt to me, if I didn't love her almost as much as I love my mom.

"Oh my god, you look so mature, Autumn," she exclaims, pulling me in for a hug, and I hug her back, loving her energy, loving being around her. I wish I didn't know her son was soon to follow, and for just a second, I allowed myself to wish that he was sick, stuck at home throwing up, missing out on this holiday just for one goddamn year.

"You literally saw me two months ago, Carol," I say with a smile as we both pull away from the hug. I look into her brown eyes as she stares at me with awe. That is just something about Carol. You can never feel inadequate in her presence. She won't let you.

"Well, time flies. I still remember when you were a baby and always wanted to be on your mom's hip," she says, giving me a small nudge with her elbow. She has this aura that holds wisdom without any judgment. She was the person I went to when I lost my virginity, crying because the guy didn't call me after he fucked me. She was the person I called when I got too drunk and didn't know where I was. I could have called my mom, who has never been strict, but still. There's something about having a trusted adult that isn't your parent that made my teenage years so much fucking easier.

I watch from my peripherals as Theo walks through my front door. My mom greets him with a hug, and I try not to let him pull my attention away from Carol. I try so fucking hard. He smiles at my mom, giving her more kindness in one gesture than he has given me over the entire course of knowing him. I nod as Carol talks to me, my attention split between her and her son.

I feel his gaze on me, and I resist the urge to look at him, not wanting to give in so soon. He probably has a cocky fucking grin on his face, like he came into this fight with more weapons than me, like he already knows he's going to win. It's that look that pisses me off every time, sending me into an angry fit, pulling every insult from my lips, but I press my lips together, desperate to keep a lid on it, and listen to Carol talk in front of me, nodding along as if I'm paying attention, hating knowing that I'm thinking about Theo at all.

My mom hugs all of the rest of the kids as they come in the house: Kylie and then Griffin, who is glued to his phone. Everyone takes off their coats and boots, dusting the snow off of them, and we shuffle into the kitchen. Everyone makes themselves comfortable, Carol putting her ingredients for to-morrow in the fridge, making room, and checking out what my mom already has prepared.

"Hey, Autumn," Theo mutters as he walks up next to me, standing close, his heat radiating from him. I hold back a grimace, hating being near him. I feel my body tune into him, disgust radiating through me, but I look forward, ignoring him completely.

I feel him stare at me, his gaze penetrating, begging for my attention, but I keep looking forward, watching my mom and Carol talk by the fridge, comparing notes for the peach pie that my mom made, a new recipe.

"Really?" Theo asks, already catching onto me, his eyebrow lifting in curiosity, a small smirk on his mouth. I feel his eyes trail down my face, taking in every inch, and I press my lips together, willing myself to keep my mouth shut. "Are we six again? Giving each other the silent treatment?" he asks with a cocky grin, but I stare ahead, feeling my blood pressure rising inside of my body, but ignoring it, knowing that we are going to go toe to toe if I give in, knowing this is going to be the longest twenty-four hours of my whole fucking life if I mutter a single word to him now.

He leans in, his body impossibly close to mine, and I feel goosebumps rise on my skin, my body rejecting the thought of even being near him. I'm shocked I don't cover in hives when he walks into the room. "That's okay, we have time," he whispers in my ear, his breath against my skin, and I turn away from him, looking to the side. I regret my movement instantly, seeing a full grin take over his face when I glance forward again. He might not have gotten a big reaction, but he got something, and I know he is going to feed off that, letting it sustain him until I give him more.

"Theo?" Carol asks, calling to the enemy, who I'm still avoiding eye contact with, ignoring his smug look of satisfaction.

"What's up?" he asks nonchalantly, still looking at me even though he is talking to his mom. I feel his eyes trail down my face, down to my neck, before he pulls them away, finally making eye contact with his mom, and I feel myself let out a breath, my resolve slipping faster than I thought it would.

"Did you grab the gravy?" Carol asks, her eyes already in a wince; she already knows the answer to her question.

"Fuck," he mutters, his voice soft, only loud enough for me to hear. I turn toward him, looking at him for the first time, and I watch as his eyes move back and forth, his brown irises looking for an answer, going back in his memory. "I can't remember," he says, his voice apologetic, and I watch as Carol just nods, not an ounce of anger in her demeanor, instantly trying to think of a solution.

"That's fine. Could you run to the store quickly? We need to grab some before the snow starts tonight," she explains, and

I watch as his shoulders sag, his immediate disinterest in going obvious. "Please?" she begs, looking at him with puppy dog eyes. She glances over at my mom for added effect, reminding everyone how much they look forward to this event. He glances at me, for just a moment, before sighing.

"Yeah, of course I will," he says with a small smile, Carol smiling back at him triumphantly.

"Why don't you go with Autumn?" My mom pipes up, my eyebrows raising instantly, my blood pressure spiking. I stare at her, waiting for her to laugh, waiting for her to take her comment back, but she just looks at me with an expectant look on her face, waiting for my answer.

When I don't reply, she speaks again. "Maybe then you can get over this stuff between you two. I'm sure we would all enjoy a Christmas without drama this year. Maybe less of a food fight," she says, a knowing look in her eyes.

Mentally, I'm shot back to a few Christmases ago, when Theo wouldn't stop fucking throwing peas at me, so I grabbed a whole ass handful of mashed potatoes and threw it at his head. It hit him right in the side of the face, forcing him to clean mashed potatoes out of his ear with a cotton swab. It was the best moment of my life, honestly, watching him scrape the food off of his face, watching the venom take over his gaze, his eyes glancing at our parents, both of us knowing we can only sling so much at each other with other people in the room. I know what he wanted to say, know how much he wanted to tell me off, but I just smiled at him, under the protection of our family, and watched as he walked away to clean up. One point for me, zero for him.

My mom has yet to forgive and forget the moment, though. She is still guarded around the mashed potatoes, convinced I'll strike again whenever I feel necessary.

"I'm not driving an hour in the car with him," I snort, laughing lightly, but my mom stares back at me, no humor in her face. I feel it start to sink in; she is actually asking me to do this, to be alone with him for a fucking hour, stuck next to him in a fucking car, both of us breathing the same air. I glance over at him, desperate for him to help, for him to fight this, but he just smirks at me, his face so fucking smug. He loves that I don't want to be around him, that he's going to have time to get under my skin, to get a rise out of me.

"I'm not doing this again. Fix whatever is wrong between you two. You have an hour to hash it out and stop making Christmas a living hell. Jesus would be ashamed of you both," she says, with a final nod, her voice stern, and I feel myself sink into myself.

"We aren't even religious," I mutter, my mind blank on things to say, on ways to get out of this. I know I'm a full-grown adult at this point, but I'm still in college, still staying with my mom while we are on semester break, and I don't want to piss her off. She can hold a grudge, and I know that if I don't do this, she is going to annoy me about it for the next month while I'm at home.

"Exactly! That's how badly I need you to work this out. You got me believing in a god I don't even agree with. Now go," she commands while ushering us closer to the door. "Leave before the storm starts," she says as we both grab our coats, dread filling my gut.

Any hope I had of this Christmas being different dissolves in front of me, a melted puddle at my feet. Things aren't going to get better. They are only going to get worse, and being stuck in a car with him is going to bring nothing but trouble. Yet, before I can argue, before I have a second to say anything, my mom is closing the door behind us, clicking the lock into place, sealing my fate.

Chapter Three

Autumn

"So are you just going to ignore me the whole time then? Is that your new way to piss me off?" Theo asks with a raise of his eyebrows, taking his eyes off the road for a moment to glance at me, his smirk making my blood boil. I push down my rage, reminding myself to hold onto my resolve, to not let this situation we have found ourselves in change anything. I still want a year of peace. I also still know he's going to do everything he can to ruin it. Nothing has changed except for our proximity, which is a nightmare that I'm currently doing my best to turn into some sort of positive, but I'm failing miserably.

I ignore him, glancing out my window, a defiant lift to my shoulders, communicating with him without saying a word, and I hate to admit it, but it feels fucking good to have the upper hand for once. He always gets under my skin, pushing and pushing and pushing until I blow up, unable to take any more of his shit, but this time, I refuse. I'm not doing that this year. Not letting him get the best of me, and it feels better than I thought. I know it's driving him crazy, this change in our dynamic, and I am soaking in the feeling, the power literally radiating off of me.

I stare out into the darkness, the moonlight glinting off the snowy streets, a little anxiety running through me when I see the snow has started already. I have lived in Colorado for my entire life, so I'm used to driving in the snow, but when I glance out my window, the snowstorm raged on, coming down hard, hours earlier than it was supposed to. This isn't the first time a storm has started early, the weather being unpredictable, and as snow blows past my window, I wonder how bad the roads are going to be on the way back. The closest grocery store is almost a half hour away since we live in such a small town, out in rural Colorado, and it's a bit of a hike, meaning we won't be home for a while, giving the roads enough time to fill with snow, making it impossible to get through. There's only so much that snow tires can do before you find yourself stuck, and I would rather not be stuck with someone I hate so fucking much. I don't want to be in this car for a moment longer than I need to be.

"The roads are fine," I hear Theo mutter, reading my mind. I turn toward him, my face in a look of disgust, hating that he can read me so fucking well, that he knows what I'm thinking without me even speaking. "I'm driving slow, it's fine," he reassures, the tiniest look of hurt crossing his face, like he is shocked that I would worry, like he is surprised that I don't trust him. I stare at him for a second, confusion wrapping around me, not understanding what he is shocked by. He is the person I trust the least. If anyone would be careless with my safety, it would be him. I can't even trust him to leave me alone, to be nice to me. I definitely can't trust him to keep me safe, to keep me from getting stuck in the middle of a snowstorm, and I don't know why that would shock him.

"Seriously? Still nothing?" he asks, looking at me again, taking his eyes off the road for only a second. I look away from him, holding onto my resolve, enjoying watching him grow more and more annoyed with me, enjoying watching the influence I have over him for once instead of the other way around.

He shakes his head, pressing his lips together into a tight line. He looks like he has to physically restrain himself from speaking to me again, not wanting to give me an inch, even though I already have a mile. I try not to smirk, desperate not to show any emotion, not to give him anything, but it's fucking hard, hard not to rub it in his smug face that for once, for fucking once, I'm winning.

The silence lasts only for a few more minutes before he looks at me again, waiting for me to break. I pretend that I can't see him, loving how upset he is getting over this.

"Are you seriously not going to talk?" he asks, his voice a huff. He says it with a roll of his eyes, but his voice holds this weird amount of desperation, which only pisses me off more. I hate hearing how badly he wants to play this game, how much joy he gets out of pissing me off. I hate knowing that he wants the upper hand again, that he's almost fucking desperate for it. I turn my head and stare at him, keeping my mouth closed, raising my eyebrows just to piss him off a little extra.

"You're such a fucking child. Giving me the goddamn silent treatment," he stews, redirecting his attention back to the road, trying to ignore me too, and failing. I watch from the corner of my eye as he fidgets, his body not used to this, not used to not being able to let off steam, to take our anger out on each other. I feel my lips turn up, and I don't even try to stop them, my urge to make this worse for him, to rub this in, overtaking me. I wonder if this is how it feels for him. If it feels like power and control to watch someone react to you. It's almost fun. It makes a few things make sense, why he likes this sick game, but it pisses me off more, disgusted that he would use me as a ego boost.

Just as I'm resisting saying something, telling him exactly what I think of him, it feels like the floor falls out from under me. My body instantly feels unstable as the car hits a patch of ice, the back tires swinging as we skate over it.

For a second, I think he is going to get control of it, think we are going to be okay, but he turns the wheel just barely, the tiniest of movements, and the car starts to spin, my heart racing in my chest as my body moves without my consent, fear wrapping around my throat, holding a scream inside. Our velocity takes us in a couple of circles until we smack into a snow bank, my neck snapping as the car finally comes to a stop, leaving us in the ditch, with the front of the car fucking buried under a mountain of snow a few feet away from the road.

My heart beats so fast I'm worried it's going to explode, worried that Theo can hear it sitting next to me. I stare out of the windshield, into the cloud of darkness, my breath coming out in pants as I try to calm myself down. It all happened so fast, fast enough that I couldn't react in the moment, but now adrenaline is coursing through me, my body shaking with anxiety. I wince as I move my neck, stiffness, and pain radiating down my shoulders.

"Are you okay?" Theo asks, his voice bringing me out of my fog, out of the shock that is running through me, and when I finally come back to the moment, I glance down, and his hand is resting against my chest, rising and falling with every breath I take. I stare at it for a second, the sight not even making fucking sense. I feel like I'm in shock, my reality not fully lining up with what I know to be true. I finally glance back at him, waiting for him to remove his hand from me, waiting for him to realize that he is touching me at all. He stares at me, not seeming to understand, a desperation in his eyes for me to answer his question, for me to finally speak to him.

I nod without thinking, knowing he needs me to give this up, to let him know that I'm fine. I can see it in his eyes, and it doesn't make any fucking sense, but I give in anyway.

He nods too, a sigh of relief leaving him, and then his eyes glance down at his hand, just noticing it, going wide instantly. Seeing what he did, he pulls his hand away quickly, like my body was hot, burning him. He glances away, one of the only times he has avoided eye contact with me, like, ever. I just stare at him, this whole situation not even feeling real.

"Sorry," he mutters, taking a deep breath, finally glancing around, looking at the damage, and taking in the shitty situation we are currently in. "I thought you were gonna get hurt," he admits, and I stare at the side of his head, trying to piece everything together, nothing making sense at that moment, my mind a fog of adrenaline and shock, my entire body seeming to be on fight or flight, and it feels like I can't process a single thing, not a word coming out of his mouth.

"It's fine," I mutter, shaking my head lightly. Silence takes over the car, and I hold back my critiques, my first instinct to cause a fight. I'm not sure why exactly I hold them back, though. I know he deserves them. If it was me who just crashed the car, just landed us in the ditch, he would tell me exactly what he thinks, tell me all of the awful things that float through his head, but I can read him too clearly. I can see all of his emotions on his face, and he doesn't need that right now. Right now, I know this has shaken him just as much as it has me, and being mean would only make it worse.

"I'm going to call my mom." He sighs and pulls his phone out of his back pocket. I wait, glancing around, trying to figure out the best move while Theo talks into the phone. Outside, my side of the car is completely covered in snow, almost up to my window, leaving me very little chance of getting out this way, but because of the way we hit the snowbank, Theo's side is mostly clear, only leaving us a foot or two that we need to walk through to make it back to the road. I sigh with relief, thankful we won't be stuck in the car or the cold for too long.

Theo hangs up the phone, sighs, and runs his fingers through his dark hair. I track the movement, my eyes searching him, waiting for an update. My nerves run through me, making my anxiety spike, making my heart beat fast. He glances at me, and our eyes connect, a vulnerability there, for both of us, that wasn't there before. We would have been fine, most likely, but this was scary. As much as I hate him, I'm glad he is okay, and I think he might feel the same way.

"She said the storm is coming in faster than expected. She is going to call a tow truck and get back to us," he says, looking at me, his eyes not wavering. The silence in the car grows thick, both of us just looking into each other's eyes, and I finally pull my gaze away, clearing my throat, glancing around the car, needing to focus on anything other than him.

The air in the car feels weird, feels unfamiliar, and I hate it. I bite my bottom lip, glancing out of my window, a wall of darkness meeting me, my own reflection looking back at me, looking like a whole different person through the glass.

"Maybe I should have driven," I say under my breath, not even thinking before I speak, not knowing exactly where my words are coming from, but I can't handle the silence. I can't handle this new territory between us. I'm used to being angry at him, and it's easier to go there instead of this, instead of sitting in the silence that feels too heavy, feels almost... intimate.

"What was that?" Theo asks. His voice has an edge that I know all to well. It almost feels good, almost feels nice to see how easily we can bounce back into the routine that we have had for years. It shouldn't make me feel close to him, but it does, giving me a sense that he understands, understands that the silence was suffocating.

"Maybe if you would've let me drive, we wouldn't be here right now," I say, looking at him with a glare. Forgetting the idea of ignoring him, my anger completely consumes me. My body needs this release, needs for us to be what we always have been to each other, a person to fight with. It's the only thing we are good at when it comes to each other.

"Maybe if you hadn't been acting like a child and ignoring me, you would've offered to drive." He challenges me and matches my anger. I sneer at him, hating that his statement holds a small fraction of truth, that I wanted to drive but refused to say anything to risk my resolve for this year's holiday feud.

"Maybe if you weren't such a dick every time I see you, I wouldn't need to ignore you." I look away from him, feeling my anger grow, clouding every other thought out of my head, reminding me exactly why I hate him so fucking much. I don't even want to be breathing the same air as him, and I hate that we are here together. I don't know what I was thinking, feeling close to him. I can't believe just moments ago, I felt glad that he was safe and alive. I wish he would fall off the side of the earth, leaving me in peace once and for all.

"Oh yeah, because you are so delightful whenever I see you. Get fucking real, Autumn. We are awful to *each other,*" he says, rolling his eyes. I open my mouth to reply, disgust ready to lace my voice, but his phone rings in his hands, and he answers instantly, cutting me off.

"Hello?" he asks when he raises it to his ear, and I just shake my head, looking out the window, desperate for an ETA on when we can get the fuck out of here and back to the comfort of my home. Maybe I can lock myself in my room, pretending to be sore from the crash. Maybe my mom will take pity on me since she is the one who forced me to come in the first place, and I can get out of this whole goddamn holiday altogether, ignoring everyone for the next thirty-six hours.

"You've got to be kidding me," he says, his voice soaking in disbelief. I glance back at him, trying to figure out what is happening. He looks back at me, shock and disgust taking over his gaze. I feel my stomach flip as I send him a glare back, my instinct telling me that whatever Carol is saying on the other end can't be good. "Okay, well, send me the address. I'll text you when we get there," he says with a sigh, looking away from me with a look of defeat, his entire body sagging. "Yep, love you too. Bye," he mutters finally before hanging up. I'm shocked to hear the words out of his mouth, not used to hearing affection, to hear kind words from him, but I push it off, remembering all the nasty things he's thrown at me, not letting this moment of intimacy change how I feel about him.

"The tow trucks aren't coming out until the plows deal with the roads. My mom said someone can come out tomorrow," he says with a tight smile, his face void of any humor. The meaning of his words doesn't fully sink in, and I wait for him to elaborate, but he just stares at me, waiting for me to understand.

"What the fuck are we supposed to do tonight?" I ask when they finally register, my voice a little too high, my panic starting to take over. Of course, I get stuck with this asshole on Christmas goddamn Eve. I tried this year. I wanted everything to be peaceful. I wanted to do my best to get through this without a fight, and suddenly, it feels like it's going to be the biggest blowout between us, like this Christmas is going to be different, but not in the way I thought. The air feels heavy with dread when he finally opens his mouth to answer.

"My mom said there is a hotel a few minutes away, and we should just stay there for the night," he says with a look of disapproval. He might think that he hates this just as much as I do, but there's no way that's true. There's no way he understands how much I fucking hate this, because this is my literal worst nightmare.

I laugh, not believing him, not trusting his words, is he trying to be fucking funny? My mind starts unraveling. I don't know if he thinks this is a good prank or what, but my brain won't allow me to believe him because that would be total bullshit. We can't be stuck together. We can't be going to a hotel on Christmas Eve, the holiday fucking ruined. This can't be happening.

He stares at me, as if I've lost my mind while I double over in laughter. My neck hurts with the movement, but I can't stop. Tears fill my eyes, my emotions getting the best of me and overtaking me without asking for my input. Theo stares at me. Pity washes over his gaze, and that sobers me up, my laugh tapering off as we stare at each other. His words suddenly feeling too real, too truthful, no longer funny in the slightest.

"No fucking way," I mutter, my voice low, disbelieving.

"You're stuck with me," he says, a small smirk taking over his face. This jerk enjoys my misery. How fucked up is it that he gets joy from my suffering? I just stare, my gut filling with a hundred emotions, disgust the predominant one.

I take a deep breath, closing my eyes, trying to calm myself down, trying not to let this ruin everything, trying to convince myself that it won't be as bad as I think, but I can't lie to myself. At least once we get to the hotel, we can go separate ways, not seeing each other again until tomorrow when the tow truck comes to pick us up.

"Fine," I spit at him. I open my eyes and give him a final nod, resigned to my fate. "Let's get this over with then," I say, shooing him to leave the car with my hand, anxious to get the fuck out of here.

He gets out with minimal problems, his side completely free of snow, but the snow comes up to his knees as he steps out, and I brace myself for the cold as I try to climb out of the passenger seat, struggling to lift myself over the center console.

"Do you need a hand?" Theo asks, his voice muted slightly by the wind blowing outside, the air stealing part of his voice. I glance up, my body positioned awkwardly as I try to figure out the best way to get the hell out of this death trap, and I scoff at him, his eyes light up with amusement and joy over watching me struggle.

Filled with a new determination to get the fuck out of this car by myself, I grumble, "Get bent." It is a little embarrassing as I have to squeeze my body into weird positions, but I finally find my way to the other side. I shiver against the cold instantly, my body not good at holding heat. I start walking without glancing back at Theo, desperate to get as far away from him as possible, wishing he would get stuck in the snow and freeze tonight.

"Other way," I hear him call behind me, the smile evident in his voice, and when I glance back, he is pointing in the opposite direction as I'm walking, and I turn quickly, redirecting myself, the snow making it hard to pick my feet up.

"I knew that," I mutter, wrapping my arms around myself, the cold already soaking through my clothes, chilling me. The walk is only fifteen minutes, but honestly, it's fifteen minutes too long to be stuck walking next to the person I despise most in this world. This is what I get for trying to do the right thing, for trying to get through this holiday in peace.

Chapter Four

Autumn

The hotel lobby is empty when we enter; only the receptionist behind the counter is present, and I take just a moment to be thankful, hopeful even, that they are going to have rooms for us, because, at this point, I don't think this day can get any worse. We need something good, because as I shake the snow from my hair, desperate for a warm bed and a hot meal, this day so far has fucking sucked. The only silver lining is that once we get into our rooms, I won't have to spend another second with Theo.

"Cam!" Theo exclaims when he takes a good look at the person standing at the front desk, obviously knowing him. The man behind the counter's uniform is crisp, the white dress shirt making him look professional, but his messy sandy brown hair and big smile make him still look approachable. How someone that looks as friendly as him could be friends with someone as fucking grouchy as Theo is beyond me, but I ignore it, just wanting to get set up in a goddamn room and out of this nightmare of a day.

"Hey man," Cam says, recognizing Theo, and I walk with Theo to the counter. Cam's eyes trail over me, a look of curiosity in his gaze. "Who's this? You finally get over that one girl?" Cam asks, his eyebrows raised at Theo, but when I glance at Theo, he is staring at me, the tips of his ears turning red, his eyes slightly larger than normal.

"Uh, this is Autumn, a *family friend*," he says with a little too much emphasis at the end, and I watch as understanding lights up Cam's face, a conversation happening between them without words. Cam nods, as if he has heard about me and knows who I am just because of Theo's description, and I raise my eyebrows in question, not even wanting to know the things that Theo has said about me, knowing they must be bad, and this guy must think the worst about me already.

"I've heard about you," Cam says, turning toward me with a friendly smile before turning toward his computer, punching a few buttons, probably looking for a reservation that doesn't exist. "You just walking in?" he asks before I have a chance to ask what he's heard, what awful things Theo has said about me.

"Yeah, we got stuck in that goddamn snowstorm and need a couple of rooms for tonight," Theo explains as he shakes the snow from his hair. I glance around the lobby, taking in the white walls and cleanliness of the place. My panic finally starts to subside. I am excited to have somewhere nice to sleep after such a disaster. I honestly knew something like this was going to happen. It always fucking does when Theo is around. He brings chaos everywhere he goes. He's like a tornado that won't get out of my life.

I look back over at Cam, waiting to see what it is going to cost for two rooms, and he looks between the two of us. After a small pause, his face turns down into a frown, and I feel my stomach sink, not knowing if I'm going to be able to take anything more today.

"Bad news," Cam says, and I feel my stomach curdle. "We only have room left," he says with a grimace like he understands how much we won't want to hear this. I watch him, waiting for him to laugh and say this is all a fucking joke. I wait for people to jump out of the office, out from behind the perfectly clean and put-together furniture, for them to all say that this whole day was a prank, but I just stand there like an idiot, waiting for a punch line that's never going to come.

"You're kidding," I mutter, my brain not even processing what this means, just that this is not the answer I want.

"The parking lot is fucking empty, man. Stop messing with me," Theo says with a huff, annoyance radiating around him, and I feel the air in the room shift, his energy bringing the entire lobby down. I turn toward him, a discreet glare in my eyes, shocked that he would talk to a friend like this, shocked that he would talk to anyone like that, but he just stares forward, a challenge in his body, his body holding all of his tension, visible for the whole world to see.

"I'm serious. We have a family reunion here for a Christmas vacation, and they all drove in on buses. They are taking up most of the rooms, so we are down to the last one," Cam says, raising his hands up in front of him as if he comes in peace, as if he is doing his best not to anger Theo but failing. I glance at Theo, waiting for him to say something, but I just watch his jaw tick, as if he is holding his words back. He is struggling and trying to be nice, so I speak instead, knowing that if I leave it up to him, he's going to be his normal dickhead self, and I'm not in the fucking mood for that.

"Two beds, right?" I ask, trying desperately to diffuse the situation, trying to get us back on track, just like I've been doing this whole goddamn holiday. I just want one year where we don't bicker the entire time, where we can be around each other in peace, and if that means I have to be the mediator, whatever. I just want to get into a warm bed and forget about this whole night, even if that means he has to be in the same room.

"Let me check," Cam says, his eyes darting back down to the computer, and I wait, trying to catch Theo's eyes. When he looks at me, I shake my head at him, trying to get him to stop being such a fucking asshole. He rolls his eyes at me, understanding my message loud and clear, probably just not caring. Typical.

"Nope. Just a king bed," Cam says, with regret and a hint of fear, and I stare at him, not believing him again.

I will myself to think for a second, desperate to find a solution, but when I glance back outside, the storm is raging on, puffs of snow blowing over the parking lot, making the entire thing look coated in white. There is a gas station across the street, and it is barely visible with all the snow blowing everywhere, and I realize that this is our last option. We can't go anywhere else, not without a car, and we need somewhere to sleep until someone can come pick us up tomorrow.

"We'll take it." I do not want to risk losing it, not wanting our one hope of a warm bed to go out the window when the next poor sap walks in the door looking for an open room.

"Are you kidding–" Theo exclaims, but I cut him off with a hand up, stopping him in his tracks.

"We have nowhere else to go. I hate this as much as you do, but I'm not going to risk sleeping on the goddamn lobby couch because you don't wanna be around me. Suck. It. Up," I say sternly, not giving a fuck if Cam has to listen to us fight. I need Theo to understand that I'm done. I've been pushed to my limit. Today has been too stressful, and I can feel myself shutting down, the desire to sleep taking over. I don't have anything left to give. I just want a warm bed and an end to this day.

"You're serious? You're okay with this?" he asks, his eyebrows raised, looking at me like I'm fucking crazy, and I roll my eyes at him, hating that he doesn't get it, that he won't just take sympathy on me for a second and just let me win. He needs to fight me every time, and it's exhausting.

"Does it look like I'm fucking okay with this?" I shriek, and I wonder how I look to him, my entire body sagging from exhaustion, my entire being so worn down that I don't even know if I have the energy to fight with him. "I'm not doing this with you. I am done," I say, my voice cracking, just barely, just the tiniest hint of emotion leaking through, and I stop talking instantly, hating the fact that he just saw me break, that he saw me hit my limit, that he saw me at the edge, emotion literally leaking from me. We go at each other so much, but we don't ever show emotion, not like that, and I don't want him to use it against me, to think I'm weak now that he has seen another side of me.

He stares at me, his face softening, and I feel my cheeks heat, embarrassment taking over. I wish the ground would just eat me up so I could stop, stop being here, stop dealing with this, stop having to think about the push and pull that comes every fucking year when he comes around.

"We will take the room," Theo says lightly, when he finally takes his eyes off of me, looking back at Cam with a new expression, one that I have trouble reading. Cam nods and starts getting our keys ready, and the silence in the lobby feels like it's going to eat me alive.

"Here are your keys," Cam says after a few seconds, giving us a customer service smile, the tiniest hint of something inside of it, but I don't stare too long, too desperate to get to the room.

We walk from the lobby, around a corner, and the elevator is right there, the door opening right for us when Theo pushes the button. We step inside and I check my key card, seeing we are on the second floor. I push the corresponding button, huffing a breath as I settle back into place in front of my biggest fucking enemy. I close my eyes, my system overloaded.

The elevator is tight, not leaving much room in between us, and I hate how close we are to each other right now, his front to my back, not pressed together, but close enough that I can feel the heat of his skin, that I can smell his cologne, a scent that *should* make me gag, but instead, it smells fucking amazing, making me want to breathe it into my lungs like an addict. I have never known what he smells like, never wanted to be close enough to find out, and I'm shocked to say that he smells intoxicating, like something I know I shouldn't have but desperately fucking want. I push that thought away, hating how out of sorts I feel, how out of control I am, even in my own head.

I feel myself frown, my head starting to pound, my body literally shutting down, and when I glance up, I can see my reflection in the elevator wall, the steel distorting the image in front of me, but I can see Theo standing close behind me, looking down at me from his height above, his head tilted so he can see just over my shoulder. He stares as if he can't look away, stares with a look I haven't seen before, almost an adoration, a lust. It makes my skin crawl. This entire night throwing me off. I'm used to our order, our systems. We have a script that we follow with each other, and this entire night has gone off of it, and it makes me nervous, makes me not know what to expect.

I stare back, my breathing coming out deep, not wanting to look away, almost not believing the sight in front of me is even real. He has never looked at me like that, like he feels anything other than complete loathing toward me, and it is making me feel weird, my stomach fluttering with every second I stare at him.

"What's got you frowning?" he asks, his breath coasting across the side of my neck, sending shivers down my spine. He smirks, staring down at me, my skin exposed to him from the collar of my coat, just an inch of my neck visible, but I'm sure he can see the effect he has on me, and I hate that.

"What doesn't have me frowning?" I ask roughly, barely trusting my voice, trying my best to keep it steady while I stare at him. This elevator feels like a different world. It feels like a place that doesn't exist outside of here. Like nothing matters, and I can do whatever I want, and that's a dangerous feeling...the feeling that consequences won't matter once we leave.

He leans down again, his lips so fucking close to my ear, and I hold my breath, waiting, not being able to predict what he is going to do, but the bell of the elevator rings, and the doors open in front of us, interrupting the moment.

"We better go find our room," he mutters so close to my skin, then straightens as the words bounce around the elevator, my body moving forward of its own accord, my legs moving while my mind feels like it's filled with fog. I let out a sigh of relief, glad to be out of there, glad to be done with that moment, but if I look hard enough, I feel the tiniest sting of disappointment too.

Chapter Five

Autumn

The room is fine: a simple bed in the middle of the room, a desk against the far wall, windows taking up an entire wall, giving me a nice white-out view of the parking lot, and a bathroom that is small and cramped but clean. It leaves much to be desired, but it looks clean and comfortable for a night, so I will take it. I'm not in the mood to be picky.

"I'm just going to clean up a little bit and then go to bed," I mutter, dropping my purse on the desk. I head toward the bathroom. I need to wash my face and clean this day from my skin. I would shower, but I don't have any other clothes, and I don't want to just put these right back on. At the least, though, I can wash my face with the tiny bar of soap and brush my teeth with the complimentary toothbrush and tiny tube of toothpaste.

I finish in the bathroom, taking my sweet time to pamper myself, knowing I need it after today, and when I walk out, I feel the dread, the realization that we are stuck in this tiny ass room for the night. I push it away, leaving the bathroom door open for him, motioning him inside. Avoidance is the best plan right now. Even though we are going to have to deal with this eventually, I'm going to push it off as long as I can.

He lifts from his spot on the bed, walks into the bathroom, and locks the door. I go to the windows, staring at the snow coming down, thinking about our car in the distance, being buried. I hope we are able to find it tomorrow, able to remember where we crashed, because if we can't, it's going to be stuck in a ditch until the snow melts.

The bathroom door opens, Theo walks out, and he plops right back on the bed, right where he was before. I close the blinds, leaving the only light in the room a few lamps that Theo must have turned on, and I stare at him for a second, starting to understand his meaning, what his body is telling me. I was hoping he would be a gentleman and would do his best to make this situation easy, to get through this night without conflict, but he is obviously going to do everything he can to make my life difficult, just like he does every fucking time we are together.

"You should call the front desk for another blanket. You're going to get cold on the floor without one," Theo says with a challenge, egging me on, and glancing back at me. I can feel that he wants a rise out of me; he wants me to react a certain way. Usually, I give it to him, playing the game that we always do, but not tonight.

"I'm not sleeping on the floor," I say simply, cocking my hip to the side, placing my palm on it. I stare at him for a few seconds, waiting for a response, but he just smirks at me, as if I'm joking. "You can sleep on the floor," I say, the silence in the room feeling like too much, my body readying for a fight.

"I'm not sleeping on the floor either, princess," he says, his eyes staring back at me, his brown irises stealing my attention. I try not to get lost in them, but feel the pull of them. It's a shame they belong to the devil himself.

"Of course, you can't just be a fucking gentleman," I mutter, hating that we are still playing this game, this back and forth. I'm exhausted trying to win against him, trying to beat him at a game that he started.

"You wanted this room. You sleep on the fucking floor," he spits out, his face contorting into disgust, and I want to retort back, keep the game going, push him until he breaks, but I take a deep breath, desperate for all of this to stop. So instead, I walk to the left side of the bed, lift the covers, and get inside, without saying a word.

"I told you, sleep on the floor," he says, his voice filled with annoyance, but I just turn away from him, not even wanting to look at him, and I close my eyes. I let the noises around me consume me, the rush of the heater, the sound of the wind outside, trying to focus on anything other than the anger plaguing me, ripping my chest apart, demanding my attention.

Just when I start to feel my body relax, to finally start to come down from the high of the day, the few lights we turned on, suddenly turn off. The heater stops too, the air in the room no longer moving. The only sound is the both of us breathing, waiting for the power to come back on. Moments pass, and nothing happens.

"What the fuck?" Theo asks from where he sits on the bed, his voice too close to me for me to stomach. I roll my eyes, not caring that he can't see me.

"It's going to come back on in a second. Stop being such a fucking baby," I retort, settling into the bed a little deeper, letting it comfort all of the stress from the day.

I wait, knowing for a fact that I am right, that the lights are going to come back on eventually, but after a few minutes, I feel myself start to doubt, start to wonder what is actually happening. The room has started to cool, just barely, the heat no longer pushing through the room. I thought the power would only be out for a few seconds, but we are still waiting, my anxiety spiking the longer the silence meets me.

"Can we call the front desk now, genius?" Theo asks, and I can hear the look on his face. I know exactly how his face is contorted, into amusement and anger, because he knows that he was right, and I hate it, hate that he has another thing over me.

"Fine," I huff, sitting up in bed, my body too keyed up to relax anymore, too annoyed and anxious and stressed. "Call the front desk if it'll make you feel better, but I doubt they can even do anything," I say, needing to be right in some way still, even if I know that I'm wrong, that the lights aren't just going to pop back on, my ego won't me admit it, instead needing him to look clueless.

This is what he does to me. Makes me feel fucking crazy, like I can't let anything go, like I have to win, and it's awful. It's not the person I want to be, but whenever it involves him, I can't help myself.

"It's ringing," Theo mutters. My head turns toward the sound of his voice, the darkness around us making me feel claustrophobic. I move off the bed, sighing, and make my way toward the windows, opening the blinds again and letting the moonlight invade the room. It doesn't do much, but it takes it from pitch black to a soft darkness where you are just able to make out shapes. I sigh with relief, a weight lifting off of my chest.

"No answer," Theo mutters, swearing under his breath. I walk back over to the bed, sitting down again, my body exhausted, my mind still whirling from the day, the chaos not seeming to let up, not seeming to give me a fucking break.

"If the power is out, do their phones work?" I ask, my mind suddenly starting to realize that this may be a longer night than I expected, that this may just be the start of something horrible. I feel my stomach sink, dread filling me.

"I don't fucking know, Autumn," Theo spits, my name an insult in his mouth. I stare at his outline in disgust, hating him, hating him with every fiber of my being. I take all my anger on this situation out on him, blaming him for every bad thing that has happened tonight, even though I know it isn't fair. I don't care about fairness right now, though. "The fucking heat went out," Theo mutters under his breath, as if he hadn't even thought that far, as if it is just dawning on him.

"Wow, you finally noticed, genius," I say, relaying the nickname back to him, loving the way I can almost feel the heat from his gaze, the daggers he is sending my way from the other side of the bed.

"I thought you were going to bed?" he asks, his voice venomous, evil. I feel myself smirk, loving the rise I can get out of him, loving the way he responds to me specifically. I've seen people annoy him, seen him get irritated with others, with his siblings, but he doesn't react to them like he does with me, doesn't let them crawl under his skin, doesn't let them know how pissed he is. With me, he shows every emotion right on his face, as if he can't help himself, and it fuels me.

"I figured you would miss my company," I reply, a smug smile on my face and I know he can hear it, even through the darkness.

"What the fuck are we supposed to do? Freeze all night?" he asks, his voice so annoyed, so fucking frustrated, and for a second, I almost feel bad, feel bad that he's going through this too, feel bad that he is just as helpless as me, but I push it away, letting my anger consume me, letting it warm me from the inside out.

"Worried you can't take the cold?" I egg, enjoying fighting with him more than thinking, more than realizing that this night just keeps taking turns for the worst. I want to piss him off, want to use him to let off steam, to let off some of my annoyance for this whole fucked up situation. I want him to pay for putting us here, even though I know it's not really his fault, but it feels better if I have someone to blame.

"You're a fucking child," he replies, his body finally settling onto the bed as he lifts the blanket, and I can feel the mattress sway under his weight, a dip forming in the middle, pushing our bodies together. "I'm not dealing with this right now. This day has already sucked enough," he mutters under his breath, sounding almost defeated. It feels weird to hear that from him, like he actually can't take anymore, but I push my sympathy away, not wanting to care about him, not wanting to give him even a fraction of my kindness.

"Fine by me," I mutter, completely turned away from him, desperate for our bodies not to touch. I would have to burn myself alive to clean him off of my skin, and I would rather avoid a painful death. "Let's just fucking go to bed and pretend this never happened," I mutter, desperately trying to find a comfortable spot, willing my mind to settle down, to calm after the events of today.

"It's fucking freezing outside. It's gonna get cold quick, Autumn," he mutters with annoyance, as if I'm not taking the situation seriously enough, as if I don't understand, as if I should be worried more than I am. I don't understand where his concern comes from, or why he is so fixated on this, but I don't dwell on my curiosity.

"Then go talk to the front desk. I'm done discussing this with you. Either go to bed or go fucking deal with it. Quit crying to me," I exclaim, letting some of my anger fly, desperate to release all of the energy that is buzzing around in my brain.

"You're such a fucking bitch, you know that?" he asks, his teeth clenched.

"I'm only a bitch to you," I reply in a singsong voice, egging him on now, the dynamic completely flipped from earlier, where he was egging me on. Now I want a fight, now I want to use each other for an emotional release.

"Don't come crying to me when you are fucking freezing," he mutters, as if he is going to have the last laugh and knows it. I snort, knowing that I would rather freeze to death than admit to him that he is right.

Chapter Six

Autumn

It did, in fact, get fucking freezing in there. Cold enough that in certain lighting, I swore I could see my breath. I was shivering, my body literally exhausted, but my mind desperately trying to stay awake, trying to keep me alive in the frigid temperature.

I try to hold out, try not to let Theo know how right he was, but it's fucking hard. I know he can feel me shaking, know he is smirking right now, the moonlight bouncing off his face. I don't look at him for long, but the second I do glance at him, wondering if he is feeling this too, I see his smug look, and that only drives me longer to keep quiet, to hold out, but it's too cold, too much for me to handle and my pride is slowly slipping away.

"God, it's fucking freezing in here," I exclaim finally, my body shivering against my commands. I can't get it to stop. I'm so fucking cold I'm starting to worry that my goddamn toes are going to fall off. No matter how tightly I wrap the blanket around myself, there's no way to warm up, to get back to a comfortable temperature.

It makes it worse that I can feel Theo next to me, feel the heat radiating off of him, feel how comfortable he is. I hate knowing this is affecting me more than him, that I'm the one who needs the heat more, that we warned me this was going to happen.

"I fucking told you," he mutters, his voice groggy, in a way that is almost sexy, but since I hate him, I find it disgusting, my mind going insane from the cold for even considering differently.

"Shut up," I say, my teeth literally chattering, the noise echoing around the room, filling the void. I try to stop, but I can't. I'm so fucking cold.

"You are the most dramatic person I know, you know that?" he mutters, and I imagine him rolling his eyes while he speaks.

"You-ou are the worst p-person I know," I reply, through my clattering teeth. I feel like I'm shaking the bed with how much I am moving. We should have talked to the front desk about the heat, but now it feels like I need to stick this out, as I desperately try to hold onto my dignity.

"Just fucking come here so you shut up," Theo says with a huff, and when I turn toward him, he is lifting the blanket, opening his arms to me, and I imagine the look of horror that takes over my face, the look of complete disgust because that is all that I feel, complete and utter disgust at even the thought of cuddling up to him, even if it is only for warmth.

"Over my dead fucking body," I say, turning back toward my side, dismissing his idea completely. No fucking way is that happening. I won't snuggle with him just because we are stuck in this goddamn hotel. I'm not that desperate, not yet at least.

"Fine, sit there and freeze. But don't complain to me when you lose a couple of toes," he says, his voice so fucking condescending, because he knows he's right, and I hate it. I'm too cold to even think of a retort, my body using all of its energy to try to stay warm.

I could go downstairs, talk to them about the heat, but I'm sure they can't do anything, can't fix something that is broken. It would only make my night worse to hear them ask me to be patient, to ask me to wait for it to kick back on. It also feels like more of a loss if I go ask, like I'm fully proving that Theo was right. I am going to do everything I can to resist going downstairs, but that doesn't mean I'm going to jump into his fucking arms.

I last about two more minutes before I let out a deep sigh and turn back toward him. He doesn't look at me, but I can feel his smug energy radiating off of him. A smirk starts to light up his face, just fucking barely, and I bite my lip, hating that I'm about to ask for the worst thing I've ever asked for. I almost don't speak, hating that smirk with every fiber of my being, but as I try to get my teeth from chattering, they won't. I finally just fucking give up, needing warmth more than I need my pride.

"I give up," I say with a huff, hating the way the words sound coming out of my mouth, hating it all, but not even caring anymore, because I'm so fucking cold I can't stand it. I don't understand how he isn't freezing too, how his body isn't shrinking in on itself, but I can feel the heat radiating off of him. I want to use him as my personal space heater, the idea of being warm right now, all-consuming. I turn toward him, hating myself for it, but my pride isn't going to keep me from getting hypothermia.

"Say please," he says, his eyes still closed, his smirk fully taking over his face now, the satisfaction radiating off of him, and I fucking hate it. If rage could heat me, I would be warmer than the sun. I stare at him for a second, wondering if he is serious, but I don't know why I even question it. Of course, he is fucking serious. It's Theo. His job in life is to piss me off.

"Get bent," I say in a huff, moving back to face my side, hating that he is next to me, hating that I got stuck in this situation, hating that I'm so helpless. I can't leave, I can't get out of this. Everything is just going wrong, and I can't do shit about it. I feel tears prick my eyes, but I push them away, desperate not to cry in front of him, even if he can't see me. I already gave him the satisfaction of giving in, I can't give him the satisfaction of making me cry too, because I know he would fucking love it.

"Okay, fine, just come here. I don't actually want you to freeze to death," he says, his voice having just a hint of comfort, but I push it away, not wanting it, not wanting him to be the person to comfort me right now. I turn over, just barely, just enough that I can see him, to see if he is serious. I don't want him to deny me again, I don't think I could handle it after such a shitty night, but when I turn back to look at him, his arms are open for me, his eyebrows raised, and although I take a second to think, to wonder if I really wanna cross this line with him, he waits for me, every bit of patience he has, he uses at this moment.

I turn back to face my side and scoot back until I can feel his body pressed against mine, him being the big spoon and me being the little one. My body continues to shiver, but I feel myself sigh with relief when my body comes in contact with his, the warmth of him comforting me instantly. He wraps his arms around me, sliding one under my neck and the other around my waist. Before I have the chance to push him off, he grabs my hands, rubbing them together in between his, heating them for me. I want to push him away, want him to stop touching me, but I don't, my body too frozen to care about anything other than getting warm, even if this is my living nightmare. At least this way, I won't lose any toes.

"We tell no one about this, got it?" I ask, my voice starting to sound normal now that my teeth have slowed their chatter. My nose is cold and I want to ask him to touch it, to put his finger on it and warm it with the insane amount of body heat he has, but I hold on to my pride, and hold back, not wanting to give him any more to hold over my head.

I hate that he is touching me, that he is feeling my ass against him, that his warmth is what I need right now. I don't want to be this close to him, to have his smell invade my senses, to feel his muscles against my waist, under my head, to feel how strong his hands are against mine, how rough they are. I don't want any of this, and I don't want my body to enjoy this, but it does. It wants to thank him, to scream how much I appreciate this. If the roles were reversed, I don't know if I would do the same thing. I would probably let him fucking freeze and enjoy every second of it.

I close my eyes then, desperate to fall asleep, desperate for this nightmare to end, to wake up tomorrow and never talk about this and to rid it from my memory with a bottle of booze. I'm going to need to shower, to use the hottest water to get his touch off of me, but I ignore that for now, deciding that it is tomorrow's problem.

I have a hard time getting comfortable. His arm under my neck isn't as comfy as it should be, his bulging forearm making my head tilt weirdly, something I refuse to admit because I know it would boost his ego, more than this situation already has.

I wiggle around, trying my best to get comfortable without removing his hands from enveloping me. They are the only thing keeping my body warm, and as much as I hate this, I can feel myself starting to get more comfortable, his body heat mixing with mine.

"Will you stop moving, Autumn?" Theo says through clenched teeth, his breath against my ear, sending shivers down my body. I hate being this close to him, hate that he is seeing me at my most vulnerable, when I need him.

I feel it suddenly, my breath leaving me as I do, a hardness against my ass, a hardness that wasn't there moments ago. I move again, convinced I'm not feeling it correctly, convinced it must not be what I think it is, but the more I move, the more I'm sure.

Theo's hard cock is pressed against my ass.

I feel my eyebrows rise, a sense of mischief running through my mind. I was so worried about him using this against me, bringing this moment up in the future, making me relive this night over and over again while he makes fun of me, but this changes things, changes the entire dynamic now. I have something over him now too, and as much as this disgusts me, I fucking love it.

I move again, feeling it rub against my ass, feeling his breath on my neck. I feel his breath hitch as I move, and I feel my ego inflate, my body filling with power. I try to tame the smirk taking over my face, loving the way his body is reacting to me even if he doesn't like it, loving that he is enjoying my ass against him, loving that his arousal is so fucking clear. I keep moving, just barely, his cock getting stiffer, and I bask in the power.

I feel fucking insane, but this entire night has been crazy, so much so that this almost doesn't feel real. Tonight feels like a dream, where whatever I do doesn't matter, where I can do everything without consequence, and that's dangerous. I know I shouldn't be moving against him, shouldn't be feeling my enemy's stiff cock against my ass, but it feels like I can do this, can make him pay for being such a dick, and tomorrow I'm going to wake up and wonder what the fuck I was dreaming because this doesn't feel like it's actually happening right now.

I wouldn't admit it to him, but my body is reacting, too. We have never been this close to each other, never had our bodies against each other like this. I hate to admit it, I really fucking hate it, but his body feels good pressed against mine, hard in all of the right places. I hate him with my entire self, so I've never wanted to admit to myself that he is an attractive guy, or that his body is built like sin, or that sometimes, when I make myself cum at night, I think of him. Not the guy who pisses me off, but I think of his body and all the ways he probably knows how to use it, all the ways he could tease me, his strong arms wrapping around me, his voice in my ear. I think of him, with my hands down my shorts, late at night, imagining all the ways our anger could be taken out on each other in much more pleasing ways than we are used to.

"If you don't stop moving, you're going to regret it," Theo suddenly mutters in my ear, bringing me back to this moment. His breath is against my neck, sending tingles down my body. I fucking hate this, hate that he has this effect over me, but my mind is whirling, thinking of my late-night fantasies, thinking of the way his voice drowns me in desire, like he is right there with me, like he wants this too, in some sick twisted sort of way.

"I don't know what you're talking about," I mutter coyly, pretending to be innocent, pretending like this isn't on purpose, but I know that he knows I'm playing the game like we always do.

But this time, he switches up the rules.

He grabs my hands quickly, giving me zero time to think, zero time to act, and suddenly they are above my head, being held together with a single hand, and when I try to pull them away, try to regain my access, he holds them tighter, squeezing them together so I can't move.

He kicks up his leg, encasing my left leg inside of his, holding down the lower half of my body. I gasp as I try to wiggle free, my mind whirling with confusion and a complete lack of understanding. One second I'm free, being warmed by him, and the next, he has me completely pinned down, at his mercy.

It's shocking and unfamiliar. I don't like it. This is not what we do. We don't do physical things. We don't make this a game of who is the strongest. We fight with words, we always have, and that's where I'm comfortable.

This? This is a new game with new rules that I don't know, and I fucking hate the fact that my body might like it.

Chapter Seven

Theo

"Do you know how long I've thought about how pretty my cock would look in your throat, shutting you up? How good you would look naked on your back, these big fucking tits on display for me?" I ask, my hand holding both of hers above her head, my leg trapping hers, leaving her completely exposed to me, her body ready to be used for whatever I want. "God, and you'd fucking like it too. I know you would because you haven't been well and truly fucked your entire life, and that's why you're such a stuck-up bitch all the time. No one has ever pleased you, ever satisfied that cock hungry mouth, but I'm sick of your attitude, so I think it's time to change that, don't you agree?" I ask through clenched teeth, my face pressed against the side of hers, and I relish the way she feels under me, against me, surrounding me.

She has been on my mind since fucking birth, her body made for mine since we both stepped foot on this planet. But, she fucking hates me, hates everything about me. She doesn't realize what she does to me, doesn't realize that she consumes my every waking thought. She thinks I hate her too, that the feeling is mutual, and she couldn't be more wrong.

I wanted to bide my time, wanted to wait until she got the stick out of her ass and stopped being such a brat to me. Still, she refuses to see what is right in front of her. I know she thinks about me. I know that I consume her thoughts too, just in a different way. She refuses to see that all that hatred she feels is chemistry just waiting for us to take a fucking chance.

I'm done waiting. I'm gonna take matters into my own hands now, and I don't really care what she has to say about it.

She is breathing hard, her chest moving with each movement, capturing all of my attention. The desire to expose her to me, to take her shirt in my hand and pull it down until her full tits are in front of me, completely consumes me, but I will myself to slow down, to take this one step at a time, because as much as I know she wants this, *needs* this, I don't want to scare her, to have her running for the hills at the end of this. Our relationship has been so full of hatred, and I don't even think she knows what a thin line hate and lust drive. She has been so convinced that it's just hate, just pure dislike for each other, and now, I know she needs time to process, to realize that there is more here than that, that there always has been.

She has been mine since she sassed me on the playground at six years old; she just hasn't known. But I'm going to make myself crystal fucking clear.

"What? You don't have anything to say now?" I ask, my voice so fucking condescending, a tone that I know riles her up. I know all the things she hates, all the ways to make her cheeks pink, to make her purse her lips, to piss her off. I know the best ways to make her mad, and now I just need to figure out the best ways to make her beg, to make her plead, to make her *cum*.

"Let me go," she gasps, her voice lacking any conviction, as if the words mean nothing. I smile, a crazy ass smile, and I know this is insane, that this is completely unlike us, but I can't help it. I've tried to wait, tried to let her come to me by herself, for her to realize the chemistry between us, but she won't budge, too fucking stubborn for her own good.

"I would if you really wanted me to," I whisper back, the smile so clear in my voice. I bring my free hand down on her stomach, just my fingertips touching the fabric of her shirt, coasting them along her waist, feeling her bare skin for the first time.

"I do," she says, her voice seething, so fucking cold, but just barely, fucking barely, unsure, like she doesn't know what she wants. Like she is caught between asking me to stop and begging me to continue.

"I've thought about this so many times, Autumn. Touching you like this, running my hands over your skin," I whisper in her ear, my voice sounding unhinged, even to my own ears, but I don't care. I have been holding back for too fucking long to sound sane right now. I've been a man deprived, and now I'm here to collect what is mine.

"You're disgusting," she mutters, her body so fucking still, as if a single movement will break the moment.

"Am I?" I ask, dragging my hand up to her chest, just barely grazing the fabric covering her tits, my fingertips just barely touching her, and when I hear her breath hitch, I know how badly she wants this, wants my hands on her, even if she has never been able to admit it, probably not even to herself.

I just keep touching her, holding her body in my arms so she can't move, loving the way her breath hitches whenever I get to a sensitive spot, as she does her best to pretend my hands don't affect her, that she doesn't care whether I stop or continue. She pretends there is nothing here, like the sexual chemistry hasn't been killing us both, but she is a liar. Now she knows it just as much as I do.

"Maybe if you say please, I'll make you cum," I tease, trailing my hand down to the top of her leggings, slipping the tip of my thumb in the waistband, loving the feeling of her body, just fucking barely, arching into me. She doesn't want to want this, but I know she does.

"You couldn't make me cum if your life depended on it," she says with venom in her voice, and I know what she is doing. She is playing the game, like we always do, egging each other on, trying to get a rise. This is where she is comfortable, where she likes our relationship. Right on the lines of lust and hate, never teetering to either end.

Fine, I'll play.

"You wanna bet on that?" I ask, my mouth forming a smirk, knowing she is going to take the bait, knowing that this is how she pretends that she doesn't want this. She makes it my idea, makes me seem like the desperate one, but I wasn't the one grinding my ass against her. She wants me to make the move, wants me to push her, and if that's what I have to do to get what we both want, so be it.

She laughs, my smirk only widening at the sound. "You don't have anything I want," she says, her head moving against my chest as she talks, her entire body exaggerated when she speaks.

"You've got nothing to lose, Autumn. Or are you a little scared that I'm going to win?" I say, pressing my mouth against her ear, loving the way goosebumps flood her skin, her entire body so fucking reactive, so responsive to me.

"I'm not scared," she mutters, but I know she is. She doesn't want to cross this boundary with me, doesn't want to actually get beyond the hate between us, doesn't want to take a chance and see what the fuck could happen between us because it's risky. Our parents are best friends, if this goes wrong, it could ruin everything. It could make every Christmas weird, every family gathering, but I don't care. I'm willing to take the risk. The question is, is she?

"Then open your mouth," I mutter.

"Wha-?" she asks, but before she can get the word fully out, I plunge my fingers into her mouth, getting them wet with her saliva, pulling them out before she can bite me, because I know her, and she would be a fucking biter if I gave her the chance.

"What the fuck is wrong with you?" she exclaims as I move my hand south, my fingers dipping under the waistband of her pants. I can feel the boundary being crossed between us, can feel the snap when my wet fingers touch her clit, even as she struggles out of my hold, as she pretends this isn't something that she wants, but I know the truth.

She wants this, almost as badly as I do.

Chapter Eight

Autumn

I try my hardest to wiggle out of his grasp, all while his fingers rub my clit, sending shivers of pleasure through me. I shouldn't want this, shouldn't be reacting this way. I should be disgusted. I don't know what is wrong with me, but I'm so horny, so fucking turned on at the way he is holding me, using my body for himself, while still trying to please me. I disgust myself and hate how I am giving him all of the power, but the smallest, tiniest part of me, loves it, giving it all to him, getting off of my mind, letting myself just react, just *be*, for two fucking seconds. I truthfully hate myself.

"Stop fucking touching me," I whisper, trying to get my voice to sound strong, not breathy, not influenced at all. The truth is, the way he is circling my clit is fucking torturous. I want him to keep going. I want him to make me cum, but I would never admit that. I'm supposed to hate his guts, not want to jump his bones.

This is not how tonight was supposed to go, not how I expected sleeping in the same bed with him would be, but here we are, his body holding me down while he rubs circles on my clit, forcing me to pretend it doesn't feel good, even though he is working my body like a fucking fiddle.

Usually, I'm hard to turn on, hard to make cum, but his movements are so slow, so fucking calculated, and my body is responding to every single stroke of his fingers, my body lighting on fire under his touch as he learns what I like, as he pays attention to every intake of breath, every movement.

"God, you like that, don't you?" he whispers in my ear, and I'm able to hear the smirk in his voice, like he has me exactly where he wants me, like he knew this would be the outcome if he touched me, like he was just holding this in his arsenal, waiting to destroy me.

"You're not going to be able to make me cum, Theo," I mutter in reply, desperately trying to will my body not to respond, trying not to show him how close I already am. Something about it being him, makes it even fucking dirtier, because I've thought of this before, thought about how our anger could translate into chemistry, thought about how sometimes when we are bickering the worst, throwing insults at each other like grenades, it feels like I want to kiss him, like I want to use his body for my own pleasure, and let him use mine too.

I always thought it was just my brain short-circuiting, not knowing who the fuck we are talking about, that he is the worst person on this planet, but now that he's touching me, I want to lean into it, let him explore my body and figure out all the ways he can bend me to his needs, all the ways I would be willing to pleasure him too, make him fucking combust in front of me. It feels all sorts of wrong, to be doing this with *him*, but I want it nonetheless.

"You wanna bet on that?" he asks again, his voice light in my ear, sending chills down my spine, and I know he notices. He always does. He sees everything. The way he has watched me, for years, like he was looking for an in, looking for some way to make me miserable, now suddenly doesn't feel so cynical, and it feels a little more erotic. I hate that I'm enjoying feeling his eyes coast down my body, leaving trails of heat in their place, making stopping points at the areas he likes most, my tits, my hips, the apex of my thighs, where his hand is now, stroking my clit like he has played with my body before, like he knows exactly what makes me tick.

"Not like I have a choice." My voice almost comes out in a moan. I just barely hold onto it, holding onto my dignity at the same time, desperately trying to hold onto my resolve, to not let him know how much I enjoy this, but it's so fucking hard when I can feel his breath against my neck, his entire body consuming mine to the point that I don't know where my limbs start and his end.

I want this, more than I should, more than I ever expected from myself, and I hate it. I hate knowing that he has this over me too, that he has my body in the palm of his hand, so I do my best to take it back, to pretend that he never had it to begin with.

"You're not as good at this as you think you are," he whispers, moving his hand down lower, one of his fingers teasing my cunt, just barely dipping inside so the tip is wet, just enough that he knows how influenced I am. I keep my reaction to myself, but I can literally feel the way he smiles, even without seeing him. It moves around the air, his smug attitude, and as much as I want to stop it, I have never been so turned on in my goddamn life.

"God, you're so fucking wet for me, Autumn," he groans in my ear. A moan takes over his voice right at the end of his words, and I try not to buckle at the sound, my eyes rolling back as he presses his finger inside of my core again, just to the first knuckle. It shouldn't feel this good, I shouldn't be reacting like this, but Jesus fucking Christ, I just want him to put me out of my misery.

I'm stubborn though, my body remembering who is touching me, that this is always a game, that he is going to use this over me, so I hold strong, desperate not to let go of my resolve, desperate to put him in his place, desperate for him to be the one that wants me, instead of the other way around.

"You're pathetic," I mutter, not trusting my voice to say more, but knowing I need to hold the upper hand here.

"What is pathetic is the way you are pretending you don't like this," he dips his finger deeper inside of me, fucking my cunt so fucking gently it makes pleasure rock through my body, my entire attention being consumed with trying to stay stiff, to not show my cards, to not show how much he influences me. "You're fucking dripping down my finger with how wet you are, soaking the fucking sheets with how badly you want this, and yet still, you can't fucking admit it, can't ask for what you obviously need. That's pathetic," he says while his finger glides in and out of me, a squelching sound bouncing off the walls, the only sound other than our breathing in the entire room.

"Why are you doing this?" I ask, a sadness in my voice, a sadness that I don't want to be there. We have been at each other's throats for so fucking long, pushing each other, taunting each other, and now all of a sudden, he wants me to beg, to tell him that I need him, and I can't fucking do it. I don't trust him, not with this. He's been my worst enemy for too fucking long. I'm not going to give this to him, he doesn't deserve it.

"Because I want you," he says simply, and it steals my goddamn breath when I process his words, his admission feeling big, feeling like too much, like it almost doesn't feel real. I don't believe that he would say that, would admit to something that I could use over him so easily, but even as I convince myself that I made it up, that my ears are deceiving me, his voice cuts through my thoughts.

"I've thought about you, naked, bared, in front of me so many fucking times, begging for me to fuck you. I've thought about the ways I could tease this tight fucking body, make it mine, and I'm sick of playing these games, Autumn. I'm sick of pretending that I hate you, when in reality, I just want to stuff my cock down your throat and make you shut up once in a while," he says in my ear, his voice soft, his words meaning nothing and everything all at once. "I think about you *constantly*, Autumn. I can't fucking stop, and I'm done pretending that I don't want this, that I don't want more between us," he says, his voice convincing, making my body feel warm, the coldness in the room suddenly gone. I soak every word he says, trying to memorize them, while chastising myself for believing him, for letting him get under my skin. I don't want to trust him, don't want to bare myself to him, to let him see me so fucking fully, but at the same time, that's all I want.

I go back and forth in my mind, not knowing what the fuck to do, not knowing if I can trust him, not knowing anything. I've told myself, for so long, that we hate each other, that he is the worst person on this earth, that I wouldn't trust him with anything, and now he's asking for everything, asking for one of the biggest things, my body. He wants everything all at once, and I don't know how I'm supposed to feel, how I'm supposed to make a decision when his finger is still pumping inside of me, my back begging to arch into him, but my mind warring with my body, begging me to be smart about this.

Chapter Nine

Theo

I keep fingering her, just fucking barely, while my words radiate through the room. It feels like torture, waiting for her reply, anxiety-inducing, but I wait silently, feeling completely fucking bared to her, completely open and honest, desperate for her to say something back.

"You hate me," she mutters, almost as if she is talking to herself, as if I'm not even here and she is just thinking out loud, as if my body isn't pressing her down, holding her against my own, while my finger fucks her cunt.

"I hate the way you influence me, the hold you have over me, but I've never fucking hated you," I whisper, my voice hoarse, my cock still grinding against her body. I am so impossibly hard, even though this conversation feels more intimate than erotic. I know what is going to come if this goes my way, if she finally lets her walls down and lets me see her fully, and I'm fucking desperate for it.

"Then why are you such a fucking dick?" she asks, letting out a shuddering breath, her cunt squeezing around my finger, her body showing me how much she likes this even if her mouth won't. It's always been this way, that her mouth won't tell me the truth, but her body will. It tells all of her secrets, even the ones she is trying to keep the most hidden.

"Because," I mutter in her ear, loving the way chills creep down her arms, and I finally thrust my finger inside of her fully, making her take it. She holds back a gasp, barely keeping it from me, but I deserve it. I want to hear every fucking noise she is holding back so I slide my finger out, and insert two this time, her entire body clenching around them, as they work slowly in and out of her. "I love the way you light on fire when we fight. Your cheeks get all red and your lips form this cute fucking pout, and sometimes, you even put your hands on your hips, showing off the curves of this fucking body," I whisper, slowly fucking her with my fingers, feeling her get closer and closer to the edge, and I keep pushing, needing her to get there with me. "Then, when I go home, I stroke my cock, thinking about the way your eyes light up every single time that I piss you off, how your body looks like fucking sin, and how you are so responsive."

I wait a beat, letting the words sink in, letting her digest them, knowing her well enough to know that she needs a second. My fingers don't stop, and I can feel that she is right on the edge of a powerful orgasm, and she's doing everything she can to keep herself from flying over. "I've been wondering if you're responsive in bed too, and I think I've got my answer, Autumn," I chuckle, her entire body stiff against mine, as if any movement will send her over, as if she can't move an inch without cumming on my hand.

I reposition, so that my thumb is hovering right above her clit, and I make her wait, letting her sit right on the edge, determined to wait until she is so fucking desperate, so needy, that she has no fucking choice but to say yes to me, until she needs me just as much as I need her.

Finally, fucking finally, I bring my thumb down on her clit. I don't move it. I don't give her the satisfaction that she needs to cum, but I feel her body buckle under mine, fucking desperate for it. She grinds against my hand, so fucking softly, as if she can't stop herself, as if she has lost control of her own body. I reach out and kiss her neck, feeling her pulse point under my lips, her pulse erratic. I taste the salty skin of her neck, desperate for more, desperate to know every inch of her body, to run my tongue along her skin and feel her shiver in response. I'm hungry for it, ravenous, and I don't think she knows how long I've been holding this back, how long I've been wanting this, to have her against me, writhing, on the edge of an orgasm.

"Just say please, and I'll make you cum," I coax. My breath against her skin, my voice so fucking tight, my cock straining against my pants, pre-cum leaking from the tip, desperate for more, desperate to hear her, to watch her unravel. "Just say please, and I'll make you cum all night," I promise, knowing that once I get a taste, once I have a piece of her, I'm going to want it all, going to need to keep her, to consume her, to make her mine in every fucking way. If she says yes, I'm not going to let her go, even if it's the last thing she wants. She belonged to me from the first fucking moment we fought and I intend to finally collect what's mine.

Chapter Ten

Autumn

I sit on the edge, so fucking unsure of what to do, my body wanting one thing, my brain wanting another, both waring with each other for power. Theo is fucking me with his fingers, so slowly, but his pacing only makes it worse, only makes me needier, more desperate for him to finally push me over the edge.

I've been sitting at the edge for so fucking long, this feels like a punishment, another way for him to get under my skin, but his words bounce around in my head, his words about wanting this, wanting me, for so fucking long, thinking about how good this would feel between us. I can't comprehend them, can't get them to make sense. It goes against everything I have believed my entire life, but at the same time, it feels right.

I've seen the way he looks at me, with heat in his eyes. I always told myself it was anger, that I was just good at pissing him off, that he just hated me that much, but I knew deep down, that there could be something more there, that there was a different kind of heat there too.

I try to grind against his fingers, forcing him to give me what I want, trying to take it from him so he can't hold it over my head, but he doesn't budge, holding my body down so fucking perfectly, keeping me where he needs me. I hold back a whine, desperate for more, desperate to finally give into him, to let him have this, but my ego holds me back, not knowing how this is going to turn out if we go down this road, if we finally cross this line.

He pumps his fingers harder, pushing me for an answer, our bodies communicating even though our tongues aren't. He kisses my neck again, his tongue darting out to taste my skin, the feeling of his mouth on me feels so fucking good, so fucking erotic that I can barely hold the whimper back, can barely keep my noises to myself.

I want to give in, want to finally jump off the cliff, see how much our anger can turn into chemistry, but god, I don't want him to have anything over me, don't want him to use this against me later, to use this to humiliate me when we are fighting again, when this doesn't work out and he throws me away, treating me like the garbage he always has. But as his fingers pump into me, using my body for everything it is worth, I realize that I hold power over him too. He exposed himself, telling me how desperately he wants me, and how much he has thought about my body. Even if this doesn't work, even if he goes back to being the biggest ass on the planet, I will forever know that he wanted me, begged for me to give into him, and he is never going to live that down.

I let myself go without thinking too hard about it, let my body sink into his, let out my first breathy moan, finally giving him what he wants, and I feel his body stiffen against mine when I do, my influence on him so fucking obvious that it makes my blood run hot.

"There's my girl," he mutters, a smile in his voice, so fucking seductive, so hot, that I'm desperate for him, desperate to feel his lips against mine, desperate to get our aggression out, to forget why we fucking hate each other and just consume each other instead.

"I thought you said you were going to make me cum," I challenge, trying to get what I want without having to say it, without giving in fully, my stubbornness still coming out to play, and I feel him pick up the pace, my body starting to deceive me, starting to believe that he's actually going to make me cum, to make it that fucking easy, but right before I'm hurdling over the edge, right when I'm gasping for my breath, my back fucking arching off of him, he stops, his fingers fully inside of me, just sitting there, filling me up and leaving me completely unsatisfied.

"You still gotta ask nicely, Autumn," he tsks in my ear, his voice trying to sound strong, to sound like he's in control, but his tone gives him away, his breathiness, the desperation leaks from him. You would only notice if you knew him as well as I do, knew how his body ticked. He wants this just as badly as I do, and we are both barely hanging on.

I swallow down my pride. My body is too needy to care right now. "Please," I finally give in, needing this more than I need to fucking breathe.

"Good fucking girl," he mutters in my ear, his voice like velvet, so fucking smooth, it almost sends me over the edge by itself. His fingers pump inside of me, going faster and faster, the sounds of my wet cunt echoing across the walls, both of us moaning, so much that the sound gets lost, my entire head spinning with pleasure.

I've never felt like this before, so wrapped up in someone, so desperate for them to touch me, to claim me, to take me for themselves. I've always enjoyed sex, liked sinking into another person, but this is different. This feels like a fucking spiritual experience, my entire soul outside of my body as pleasure wraps around my spine, taking me hostage.

"God, your pussy is clamping around my fingers," Theo groans into my ear, his voice hoarse, like he is barely hanging on, like he is just as turned on, just as out of his body as I am, as if my pleasure is his, as if we are connected on another level.

My orgasm rips through me, my back arching, my pussy pulsing, my tits begging to be touched, my entire body on a high that I've never experienced, as pleasure consumes me, my moans taking up all the space in the room, my mind not even conscious of the sounds I'm making. I lose control of myself, getting lost in the pleasure, and he seems to too, enjoying watching me fall apart just as much as I enjoy falling.

I come down slowly, my breathing fucking erratic, my mind racing, trying to figure out what this means, trying to figure out how someone I hate so much can bring me so much goddamn pleasure, while my mind is still fuzzy as hell, the orgasm wiping out half of my brain cells.

Theo keeps fingering me, slowly, so it isn't too intense, so it doesn't start to hurt with how fucking sensitive I am, wringing every ounce of pleasure from me, taking it all for himself as he kisses my neck, his groans absorbing into my skin.

"Jesus Christ," I mutter when I feel as though I can move again, my body coming back to me, the pleasure just a distance throb. I try to catch my breath, my entire body desperate for oxygen now that the pleasure is gone.

Theo just keeps kissing my neck, as if he can't get enough, as if he wants more, as if he doesn't want this moment to stop, and I feel my body come alive again, somehow, wanting more too, desperate for another round with him.

"God, that was so fucking hot, Autumn," he mutters into my skin, and I feel it roll over my body, his words sinking into my skin. I feel myself smile, loving the praise he gives me, loving the way it makes me feel, but it's also a reminder, of who this is, who is wrapped around me, who just consumed my orgasm, stealing it for himself, and I feel myself start to shut down, my anxiety ripping through me, like this is too good to be true, like I shouldn't be trusting him with this part of me.

I pull away, needing to get away, the cloud of pleasure disappearing within a second, my need to pull back into myself outweighing how good it feels to be in his arms. He doesn't see my movement coming, so I pull away from him without any resistance, but I hear his small intake of breath as if I've shocked him.

"Let me go," I mutter, my voice cold, my entire being feeling too exposed, too vulnerable now that I've let him see that side of me, now that he knows what I look like when I cum, when I'm my most vulnerable. I can't bring myself to regret what happened, but I hate the way it has sliced me wide open, for him to see every piece of me so clearly. Post orgasm, it doesn't feel as good to be looked at so openly by someone who I have hated for so fucking long.

"Hey," he soothes, as I scoot away from him, my body caving in on itself, my arms going around my legs as I sit up, smoothing down my hair, trying to make myself look presentable. He comes closer and I look away, not ready to look him in the eyes, not ready for him to see me again after that, to see the vulnerability so clear on my face.

"I shouldn't have done that," I chastise myself, not knowing what to do, not knowing how to come back from this. I think of all the ways he will use this against me, all the ways I will come to regret this later on, in the light of day, in front of our moms, how he will make me feel humiliated over and over again about this. I know I'm spiraling, making this into a bigger thing than it needs to be right now, but I feel deranged, like rational sense means nothing.

"Autumn, do you know what you fucking do to me? How fucking often I obsess over you?" he asks, his voice pleading, desperate for me to understand, and I glance at him, my anxiety feeling just a tiny bit smaller at his admission, like he is exposing himself just as much as I have.

"Theo, we fucking hate each other," I mutter, his words not connecting with reality, with the way we have treated each other for so long. We have been fighting forever, picking on each other, getting under each other's skin, desperate to get a rise out of one another. I have hated him, claiming him as my worst enemy for so fucking long. This doesn't even feel real. His words feel like a myth, something that doesn't even make any sense.

"No, you hate *me*," he says, his words sounding so fucking sincere, they steal all of my attention. "I haven't hated you for a fucking second. I have been worshipping the ground you walk on since you were a brat to me at six fucking years old. I have wanted a rise out of you, loved pissing you off, that is true," he says with a shrug, his mouth forming that fucking smirk that has pissed me off for years. "But, I haven't hated you, I just wanted to influence you, to get a reaction, because you are on my goddamn mind so often. You consume me, Autumn. My every fucking thought, all the time, and I hate the idea that I'm nothing to you." He looks away, as if he is embarrassed about what he is going to say next. "It's easier to be your enemy than it is to be invisible to you," he says, his voice low, as if he isn't sure of his words, of the truth coming out of his mouth.

I stare at him, my mind so fucking blank, his words not even making sense, but at the same time they do. They make all of the sense in the world, like this something we have been walking around for so long, like this was always going to happen. Like it was more a matter of when not if. I stare at him, his words absorbing into my skin, taking up space in my body, committing themselves to my memory, and as I stare at him, I start to fucking believe him, my entire perception of our relationship shifting in a matter of moments.

"I am so fucking hard for you, Autumn, so fucking turned on that it fucking *aches*, for you. It's only for you. My cock responds to no one else, other than you," he mutters, coming closer to me, his body magnetic pulling me toward him, his mouth inches away from mine, so close that our breath starts to mingle. I stare into his eyes, watching him take in every part of my face, as if he can't look away. I watch as pure desire, pure desperation takes over, his entire expression written out, telling me every secret he has ever had, giving me every fucking piece of him.

In an act of complete impulse, I reach down, needing to see the truth for my own eyes, and unbutton his pants as he lays back, his eyes wide. I push the waistband down as his head hits the pillow, needing to see his cock, to feel the heat from him, to feel the softness of his skin against mine. He lifts his ass helping me, his hands franticly trying to push them down faster. He wants this as badly as I do, needs me to touch him.

His cock bounces out as his pants and boxers inch down just enough to release it. I reach out, my hand on his thigh, and I inch my way up, so slowly, wanting him to tell me to stop, to tell me this is all a fucking joke, to confess that he's been lying this whole fucking time, but as I inch closer to his cock, I just watch his face become more desperate, more needy and it fuels me, pushing me farther, pushing my anxiety away and letting my courage take over, my need to find out how truthful he is.

The tips of my fingers finally touch his cock, and I take his length in my hand all at once, needing to feel all of him, needing to feel his truth as a physical representation instead of words, and I feel a gasp leave my lips, so quietly, but the room is silent, so it bounces off the walls, stealing both of our attentions.

His cock is hard, so fucking impossibly hard in my hand, and I stroke it with a firm grip. He's big, bigger than I've ever had, and I feel my mouth water at the thought of taking him inside of me, letting him fuck my mouth, my throat, my cunt, allowing him to split me in half and have his way with me while his cum fills every single one of my holes.

"You can't do that for long or I'm going to cum, Autumn," he groans, his voice so fucking hoarse, so needy, and my eyes dart to his, my tongue darting out to lick my lips, and his eyes track the movement, his eyes glued to me, as if I'm the object of all of his desires, as if he can't look away while I touch him. It urges me on, his pure desire for me, makes me bold, makes me believe every word he has said to me tonight, makes them feel like fact and less like fiction.

His skin is soft and impossibly hard in my hand, as if he is just seconds away from exploding. His cock leaks precum, the sticky liquid coating the head of his dick as he lets out a gust of breath, a guttural moan. His noises just make me needier, make me want to do more, make me want to see how far I can push him, just like he pushes me.

"You have to stop, Autumn," he mutters, his voice a croak against his lips, but I just look up at him, our gazes crashing together, and I watch as his face turns from pain to bliss, watch as he lets go of every ounce of control, watch as he succumbs to the pleasure the same way I did. I watch as he cums in front of me, his entire truth written out on his face, and I keep stroking his cock, my hand catching all of his cum as I move, a squelching sound filling the room as the liquid is just used as lube while I continue to jerk him off. "Jesus fuck," he mutters when he has finally caught his breath, when he has come back into his body, and I just stare up at him, feeling so fucking powerful, amazed that I could make him cum so quickly, make him feel so good, and honestly, all I want is to do it again.

Chapter Eleven

Theo

My cock is still wet with my cum, my last orgasm working its way through my body, and I expect her to give me a break, to let me make her cum again, to let me feel her clench around me, and honestly I'm desperate for it, but instead, she leans down, her eyes never leaving mine, taking my wet cock in her mouth, tasting my cum, bringing it to the back of her throat, until she is gagging, her eyes forming a wince as my cock bottoms out in her throat. I feel pleasure start in my spine all over again, my body so fucking tuned into her, so fucking desperate for everything she is willing to give. I need all of it.

"You are pure fucking sin, Autumn," I moan, not allowing my head to tip back like it wants to, not giving up a second to look at her with my cock in her mouth, not wanting to look away for even a moment, knowing I can't miss this because the sight in front of me is so fucking pretty. It's something I've wanted to see for so long, and I'm worried if I look away, I'll wake up from yet another dream, my cum soaking my boxers instead of her mouth.

"I thought that was what you liked about me," she mutters, her tongue darting out to slide down my cock, pleasure wrapping its way around my spine as she moves. I feel consumed by her, her smell, her aura, her entire being, the only thing my mind can even think about, the only thing my brain will let me see, because that's what she is, all fucking consuming. She has consumed my thoughts for so long, and now that she's here, trusting me with this, I can't fucking help but feel like it's a dream.

I want to be inside of her, want to feel her wrapped around my cock, want to feel her clench as she cums, squeezing my dick until I cum inside of her, but I can't seem to move from this spot, can't seem to ask her to stop, not while her cheeks are hallowed out as she sucks the tip of my dick into her mouth, the lightest fucking smile on her face as she does. She is finally seeing what she does to me, finally starting to understand how much influence she has had on me for so fucking long, and she loves it, loves the way my body responds to her.

"God, you're too fucking good at that," I groan with pleasure, my voice hoarse, my orgasm already starting to bloom at the bottom of my spine, my balls aching to fill her mouth with cum, to make her take my load and swallow it like I know she will. I want my cum inside of her, our DNAs to be combined. I need there to be evidence of tonight because I don't know how this is going to end. She just started trusting me, just starting giving me pieces of her that she wouldn't have dared to give to me before, and I don't want to lose this, lose what we found in this room, lose the way she is looking at me, like she knows I'm wrapped around her fucking finger.

"Autumn, baby," I beg, my voice a fucking plead as she takes my cock into the back of her throat again, gagging, giving me everything she has, but it's too much. I can't handle this for much longer without lining her throat with my cum. "I'm going to cum again if you keep going," I whisper, not really wanting her to stop but knowing she needs a warning of how fucking close I am.

She keeps going though, not letting up, not for a fucking second, taking my cock into the back of her throat over and over again. I groan, feeling for the first time tonight, that I'm not sure if I know what I got myself into, that I might be in over my head, with someone who knows how to please me even more than I know how to please myself.

"You gotta let me cum in your mouth, baby. I'm so fucking close, and I need to cum," I rush out, my voice begging her, desperate to feel her wrap around me and take every fucking inch while bliss rolls over my entire body. She stares at me with a devilish look on her face, and I stare back, loving this side of her, loving knowing that she is playful and fun even when I'm two seconds away from cumming, that she loves keeping me on edge, watching me become fucking desperate for her, more so than I usually am.

"Say please," she mutters, her tongue darting out again to slide down the underside of the head of my cock, the grin present on her face while she teases me, making my head fall back as I try to get myself to say the words, my ego standing right in the way.

It's easier to be the one wanting her to beg, to be the one with all of the power, to be the one keeping her on the edge. I like holding control, having her exactly where I need her, but this, this feels different, like it's a bigger deal, like I'm finally showing her my hand, showing her how badly I have wanted her for so fucking long. I have thought about expressing this to her a hundred times over, and the idea of finally doing it, finally letting her know how badly I need her, seems like more than I was ready for when I walked into this room tonight.

But I'm not an idiot. I have her, for now, at least. While we are in this freezing cold fucking room, in this bed, she is mine, and I'm not going to lose this, not going to stop it before it has even had a chance to bloom. I'm not going to walk away from her because I know she is two seconds away from running from me, and one of us has to hold the other one down, grounding us both.

I look back at her, her mouth still on my cock, keeping me right on the edge, but her eyes speak to me, showing a tiny amount of vulnerability, like she is worried I'm going to let her down, like she worried that her trust shouldn't be placed in me, and I want nothing more than to prove her wrong.

"Please," I beg, my hips thrusting, just fucking barely, my body moving on its own accord, desperation soaking into my bones. "Please let me cum in your mouth, Autumn. I fucking need it." I thrust into her mouth, my cock barely moving an inch, but it feels like fucking heaven, the heat of her mouth making my pre-cum leak from my cock like a fucking facet, and she just swallows it down, taking it so fucking well. "I fucking need you, Autumn. Fucking please," I beg, letting go of my ego, letting go of the hope of holding onto my dignity, not caring when it comes to her. I will give her everything, will give her my all, if only for the rest of the night, if only for the time she is willing to give me, because I have wanted this for too fucking long to back down now, to let fear stop me.

She sucks, her cheeks hollowing again, the sight almost sending me over the edge altogether, but she holds steady, her mouth barely moving, her tongue sliding over the head of my cock, teasing me, and she waits, looking at me like she expecting something, and it takes me a second before it clicks, but the second it does, I thrust my hips up, so fucking slowly at first, not wanting to hurt her, but it's almost painful, holding myself back, because I want nothing more than to use her mouth as a fuck hole, claiming her for myself.

"Oh god," I groan, as she takes every fucking inch, my cock in her throat, stealing her oxygen. "Good fucking girl. Good fucking girl, don't stop," I mutter, not even really knowing what is coming out of my mouth, just fucking talking, pleasure consuming my every brain cell. "Please don't stop, please don't stop," I beg, my hips thrusting faster, fucking her throat, forcing tears into her eyes, the sight so fucking erotic. I watch her swallow my cock, her eyes holding more heat than I've ever seen in my life.

My movements become erratic, so desperate, so fucking needy, and she takes every thrust, chokes on my cock like she needs this as badly as I do, like this pleases her too, like she is getting off on this, on watching me come apart.

"I'm gonna fucking cum, Autumn," I groan, my voice a plea for her not to stop, my voice so fucking breathy and desperate. I should be embarrassed, but I can't bring myself to feel anything other than the pure pleasure, the pure delight of fucking her tight little throat, of knowing that she is letting me control this, letting me use her body as I need to.

Cum shoots out of my cock, coating the back of her throat, and I watch as her eyes widen as my load shoots, groans leaking out of my mouth, my body fucking shaking with desire, my orgasm literally ripping through me, completely consuming me, the only thing on my mind is her, the only thing I can think about, smell, watch, is her.

She swallows me down, taking every inch of my dick even as I cum in her mouth, and then she swallows that too, her throat physically gulping, and it makes my cock twitch on the way out of her mouth, my cum and her spit mixing together, my cock glistening in the moonlight, and I know I'm going to be hard again in a matter of seconds, this moment playing on a loop in my mind forever.

I push my pants down all the way, watching them drop to the floor, and then I make a show of pulling her pants off, desperate to expose her to me, needing to feel more of her, to have her wrapped around me. I then pull her up to me so she is straddling me, lining her body up with mine so her weight is on top of me. I need to feel her, need to know this is fucking real, and I slam my lips to her, needing to taste us, needing a physical representation of us together. I groan into the kiss, my tongue darting into her mouth, and she sinks into it too, her entire body melting into mine, and my hands start to find their way to her cunt, desperate for a feel.

My fingers climb up her thighs, barely teasing her, my patience too fucking thin, and when I finally slide a finger inside of her, she is so fucking wet, practically dripping on me. I groan into our kiss, sliding another finger inside of her, loving the way she gasps into my mouth, letting me consume her moans as I finger fuck her, her pussy so fucking willing, so responsive to me.

"Fuck," she mutters, leaning into me, leaving her face close enough to mine that I can't see her, but I feel her clench around me, her orgasm already close. My cock hardens instantly, thinking about her enjoying giving me head, enjoying it so fucking much that she's already close to cumming again for me, already close to claiming her own pleasure.

"Cum for me," I demand, my voice no longer needy, no longer begging, now a force, knowing that I need to see her cum again, knowing that I need her to fall apart on top of me, while my cum is still wetting her lips.

I slide my thumb against her clit, making small circles, pulling moans from her. She is so close to my ear, my entire mind filling with her, once again, taking up every fucking brain cell in my head as she moans her wetness running down my fucking fingers with how drenched she is, and I feel her clench, her body spasming as her orgasm takes her over, as her body listens to my demands. I moan too, my entire being so fucking turned on, even though I've already came twice, but I can't believe she was that horny, that close to cumming again already, just from having my fucking cock in her mouth.

It's a confirmation that I didn't know I needed, that this obsession, that this crazy chemistry between us, is mutual. I knew it was, knew she thought of me just as much as I did her, just with hate on her mind instead of lust, but there was a fear, an uncertainty, that I was making it all up, making my reality what I wanted it to be. I followed my instincts, desperate to be correct, desperate for the truth, and having her in front of me, her cum running down my fingers, calms me more than I would care to admit.

She comes down slowly, her body pulsing with pleasure and I do my best to wring it out of her, wanting more and more and more. I could make her cum all day, spending all of my time with my fingers inside of her, with her moans filling the air.

"Holy shit," she mutters in my ear, finally opening her eyes and lifting her head so that she can look at me, our eyes connect, and it feels like I'm looking at a new person, like the last few hours have changed us both, no longer the enemies that hate each other, that bicker, but now we've found common ground in each other, and I feel my heart swell, loving the way that she is looking at me, no longer with disgust, but with mischief, with lust, with almost an adoration, if I look hard enough.

"I'm gonna need to fuck your throat more often," I mutter, nipping at her jaw with my teeth, needing her skin on mine, needing us to stay connected. She laughs a little, her forehead sweaty, her hair a fucking mess, but she looks so beautiful, and I kiss down her neck, needing my lips on her more than I need to breathe.

"Yeah, I think I liked that a little," she mutters, her voice tired, relaxed, and it's the first time I've ever heard her sound like that, so fucking calm, not at all agitated. She leans into my kiss, exposing her throat to me, and I take full advantage, biting and sucking, committing every inch of her to memory.

I run my hands up her waist, exposing her stomach by lifting her shirt over her head, feeling her skin under my hand, skating them up so fucking slowly, teasing her, as if we haven't done enough of that already. I unhook her bra, so slowly, so fucking carefully, and it falls away exposing her tits to me, to the cold air of the room. I watch as her nipples harden, and I lose every other thought in my mind.

I lift myself up, just enough to rip my shirt off, the only thing holding us back from being naked, from being completely exposed to each other. I'm desperate for it, to feel her skin against mine, to warm her body up, to keep her tight against me, never letting go.

I'm feeling lazy now, after both of us cumming twice, and I want to take my time with her. I want to explore each other thoroughly, especially with the threat of tomorrow coming. I'm not sure what it is going to bring, if this is going to change things for us or not.

I hope it doesn't, change things that is, or I guess, I hope it does. I hope things are different between us, more like this. I want things to be easy and carefree, but I can't say I'm not worried, can't pretend that there isn't anxiety running through me, at the idea of her thinking this was a mistake, thinking this shouldn't have happened. I know her, better than she thinks I do. All of the time that she has spent hating me, I've spent studying her, taking in every inch, every expression, committing them to memory, and I know she is going to be scared tomorrow, going to want to run, but I can't let her do that. After tonight, there isn't going to be a possibility of this stopping here, of this night being a one-off thing, because I'm becoming addicted, addicted to having her skin against mine, to owning her moans, to claiming them for myself. I have just started to get a taste, we can't stop now.

I take my time kissing her, my lips finding their way back to hers, and I just let her consume me, let her mouth explore mine, let her find her own rhythm, while I sit back and enjoy, loving the comfort between us.

I run my hands along her body, urging her on, desperate for more, but I do my best to hold back, needing to give her a chance, a chance to be bold, to figure this out for herself. To figure out that she is mine, that she isn't going to be able to walk away from this. I need her to want this, just as badly as I do, and she does. I fucking know it, but she needs to realize it too, needs to come to terms with it.

Her mouth latches onto mine, her kiss desperate for more. Her body grinds against mine, finding her pleasure, and she sinks into it, this thing between us, letting herself feel it, letting herself get wrapped up in me.

I feel her get impatient, wanting me to make a move, wanting me to progress this thing along, but I just kiss her, loving the feel of her against me. This is something I have thought about for so fucking long, something I have stroked my cock to the thought of, countless fucking times, imagining what it would feel like to have her tight body pressed against mine, her hands in my hair, on my chest, exploring my body.

She makes this little whine in the back of her throat, a sound of impatience, and I groan into her mouth, my cock stiffening again, not caring that I've already came twice, not caring at all when she is involved. I just need more, need more constantly when it comes to her, and I want her, want to be inside of her, fucking finally, but I can't do this without her knowing what it means, how big of a deal this is.

I pull my mouth away, keeping our foreheads pressed together, and her eyes flutter open, vulnerability and fear, sitting right there for me to see, and I stare back, giving her everything I have, giving her my body and my fucking soul, as if she hasn't owned it for her entire life.

"You can't get scared of this tomorrow," I mutter, my voice barely a whisper, my worst fears finally surrounding me. "I've wanted you for too fucking long to let this go. I'm not going to. You've been on my fucking mind for years, and you can't walk away from this, not after tonight." I stare into her dark eyes, the moonlight barely giving me anything to look at, but I see enough to know she is taking in my words, really letting them sink in, because I feel her fear radiate off of her, her vulnerability consuming her. I wait, just staring at her, desperate for her to agree, to let me claim her, but the longer the silence fills the room, the more my anxiety starts to eat me alive.

Chapter Twelve

Autumn

I stare back at him, my heart beating out of my fucking chest as I process his words, as I try to compare them to my own reality, and it doesn't make sense. I have hated him for so long, have seethed at the thought of his name. I shouldn't feel these things between us, shouldn't want him inside of me, shouldn't want to watch him fall apart while he fucks me.

And I definitely, shouldn't want to do it again tomorrow, to walk out of here together, trying to figure out what the fuck this is between us.

Because I do have to admit, there is something there, some kind of insane chemistry, something tethering us together, something between us that feels too big, too scary, like it could consume us, ruin us, and that fucking scares me. That's why his words hit me right in the chest, because he knows me so well, knows my fears before I seem to.

I do want to run, want to soak this up tonight but run tomorrow when the light of day hits. I want to give this to myself, let myself sink into him because, in the back of my head, I know this is fragile. I can be brave tonight, and tomorrow, I can walk away from him, pretending that I don't feel it, pretending that his confessions don't influence me, that he didn't turn my entire world on its axis when he confessed to having feelings for me, for being consumed by me.

I battle with myself, not knowing if I want to give myself to him, if I want to commit to this. It already feels like too much, like I've exposed myself too much already, like I already want to take this all back, but at the same time, this feels better than I ever expected. I didn't expect for us to have real chemistry, for his words to have power over me, to love the way he looks when he falls apart, and enjoy letting him watch me fall too. It's scary, scary because I have hated him for so fucking long, but it also feels right in a way I never expected, and that makes me want to leap, want to jump into him, and throw caution to the wind, letting my impulsivity take over, but I hold myself back, not knowing if I can trust him, not knowing if I want to.

"Say something," he begs, his voice so fucking quiet, I almost don't hear it. I stare into his brown eyes, trying to find answers to all the questions, to all of my concerns and fears, and he stares back at me, a look of longing, a look that has been there longer than I want to admit. I've seen it before, I just didn't register what it was, didn't understand what it meant, but now it is clear, the desire taking over his face makes sense, it matches his words.

"I don't know what to do," I admit, giving him the truth, needing him to see inside of me, to see my thought process. "You are the person I trust the least. I have hated you for so long, and now you are confessing to this, and I feel it," I mutter, leaning into him, letting my body inch closer, our lips only a breath away. "I feel what there is between us, the chemistry that has been hiding right under the surface." I close my eyes, not wanting to look at him when I say the next part. "But I'm scared, because I don't trust you, not yet, and I don't want to give this to you and have it all be a joke, have it all be a prank to get me to be vulnerable so you can use it against me," I admit, keeping my eyes closed, waiting for him to speak. When he doesn't, I open my eyes, so fucking slowly, letting him come back into focus, his eyes staring back into mine, a look of determination in his gaze.

"I would never, Autumn," he says, his voice hoarse. "I know I don't deserve your trust, don't deserve for you to give this a chance, but I want you," his voice gives way to his desire, his cock rubbing against me, under me, and he lifts his hips as he speaks, his body giving way to his words. "I want this. I want you. I've wanted it for so fucking long, and I thought you knew. I thought you knew how desperate I was for even an ounce of your attention," he admits, my resolve starting to deflate, my fears seeming to be answered with his confession. He talks so sincerely, like he is willing me to understand. I stare back at him, letting his words soak into me, letting them become truth, and I let myself imagine what would happen if I let the fear go, and I did exactly what I wanted. I let myself imagine how good we could be, how much there is between us. I don't hold myself back, don't tell myself that I'm being foolish. I just let myself imagine, letting go of every ounce of fear and just letting myself fall, throwing caution to the wind, giving myself over to him.

"Kiss me," I beg, my voice needy, desperate. I grind against him, letting my body talk for me, letting my body express everything I'm feeling. At first, I'm worried he isn't going to get it, that he's going to make me say the words that I know I can't. It's too much too soon, and if he asks me to say it, I might back down, might lose my courage, but I just watch as a smile takes over his face, understanding dawning on him, and his lips smash into mine. A sigh of relief escapes my mouth as he consumes me, as he takes me for himself, his hands exploring my body.

I feel the change in him, feel when he finally lets himself go, lets himself ravish me. He touches me and worships me like he has meticulously thought this through and knows exactly what to do next. His words ring true in his actions, his hands telling me all of the things he hasn't said, all of the things that I don't know if I can believe. His touch is light, light enough that it sends goosebumps down my back, but it feels so fucking good. He runs his hands up my sides, teasing me, making me think he is finally going to touch my tits, only to run back down, keeping me on edge. He does this while he kisses me, his mouth consuming my every thought, making it hard to fucking think. His tongue coasts against mine, making my core fucking shake, my entire body just turning to a puddle of need, a puddle of desire, only for him.

I feel him move his arm, his hand leaving my body, and I try not to react, but I whimper, the sound leaving me just barely, his mouth consuming most of it, and I feel his lips form a grin against mine, his delight at my reaction so evident, but

I don't feel embarrassed, don't feel shame for the fact that he has this impact on me, instead it pushes me closer, my entire body desiring this, so fucking needy that I feel as though I can't breathe.

He slides his hand in between us, lining his cock up to my entrance, and I gasp lightly when the head of his dick presses inside, just barely, barely even moving a goddamn inch, but my body is on fire with desire, so fucking tuned into what he is doing, so tuned into his movements.

He pushes further inside, his hand coming back to my side, and this time, as he thrusts inside of me, his fingers skate over my nipples, his tongue against mine, and I feel an orgasm start to bloom, my body alive as he hits every single nerve ending.

He fucks me slowly, barely inching his cock inside of my cunt as his mouth consumes me, his fingers playing with my nipples, kneading my skin. He groans into my mouth, his body starting to shake under me.

I already know how this feels for him, because it feels the same way for me. This is overwhelming, intense. I didn't realize my body could feel this good. I didn't realize I could be this close when he isn't even fully inside of me yet, but I am. I am so turned on that I can't think of anything else. I can't process a single thing until he wrings the pleasure from me, taking every ounce for himself, and I know he feels the same way, feels this chemistry between us, feels the connection that I have thought was hate for so fucking long.

I adjust myself on his cock once it's fully inside, moving my hips barely, trying to get comfortable with his full length inside of me, his cock stretching me to the brim.

"Fuck," he mutters, his voice hoarse as he pulls away from our kiss. He sucks in a breath of air, as his eyes dart down to my pussy, to where we are connected. I watch as he takes me in, naked on top of him, my body on full display for him. "There's no way I'm gonna fucking last long like this," he says, his eyes not even holding contact as his gaze gets stolen by my body, as if he can't help himself, as if I am an addiction that he can't seem to let go of.

"Me neither," I reply sheepishly, looking down at him as he tries to hang on to his control, trying to keep himself from cumming inside of me. His face contorts in pleasure as my words settle. I move my hips, bouncing just slightly causing both of us to moan as I move. He feels so impossibly fucking good. His cock fills me completely and steals my fucking breath. His hands grab my hips, hard enough to put bruises on my skin, but I fucking revel in it, enjoying the way he feels about me and how easy it is for him to be so out of control.

So easy for him to give me everything. He wants this so desperately, he can barely hang on, can barely stop himself from cumming inside of me, and I am loving every minute of it.

"Jesus Christ," he says as I place my hands on his chest, using him to balance me as I lift my ass, sliding up and down on his length, going so slowly, trying to keep him on edge, trying to memorize the look of bliss on his face as his head tips back and his eyes close, focus and determination taking over his expression.

"That feel good?" I ask softly, my skin slapping against his, the sound echoing in the room. It shouldn't turn me on, shouldn't bring me closer and closer to orgasm, but it does. I am consumed by him, every single one of my senses being engulfed by him all at once, and it's so overwhelming.

"Yes, yes, yes," he repeats without reason, his words tumbling together, and I smile, pushing my arms together causing my tits to press together in front of him, and I watch as he looks up at me, complete awe on his face, and I feel my orgasm barrel through me, completely taking over my body, shocking even me. My mouth falls open, pleasure taking over me before I can even say anything, but I know he feels it because when my hips stop moving, my legs seizing up and shaking around him, he grips my hips, thrusting into me, fucking me with all of the force he can, his pace relentless as his head tips back again as he tries to hang on while I squeeze around his cock, my pussy pulsing with pleasure.

"God, you're so fucking tight, Autumn," he mutters through clenched teeth as my orgasm ebbs, small shocks of pleasure still running down my spine, my entire body feeling like a live wire, so fucking sensitive. I feel like I'm having an out-of-body experience while being right there, more present than I've ever been, all at the same time.

Theo moans, pulling me out of my thoughts, his groans of pleasure sounding too fucking sweet, his use of my body destroying any resolve that I had that this wouldn't work between us, that this isn't real. This pleasure, this feeling right here, right between us, is the realest thing I've ever fucking felt, and I know he feels it too.

I see the moment he breaks, where his pleasure takes over his body, his entire being consumed by it, completely and utterly taking hold of every piece of him because he moans loudly, the sound echoing across the room, his thrusts losing their tempo and becoming sporadic, as if he can't control his body anymore.

He flips me onto my back before I have a second to process what he is doing, his body suddenly towering over me, a picture of strength. His cock thrusts into me hard, giving me his all, pumping me so fucking full of his cum that I start to wonder if it's going to leak down to my ass, claiming every single part of me all in the same night.

I grip the sheet next to me, pleasure soaking into my bones as he fucks me, my entire body wanting more and more and more, never quite having enough of him. It feels like now that I got a taste, now that I have seen what could be between us, I don't know how I'm ever going to be without it, to be without this.

He pumps into me, his body using mine greedily, taking whatever he can from me, soaking me with his pleasure, with his cum, forcing me to take it, but I'm completely willing, almost desperate for it. He fucks me, his cock thrusting inside of me, his body giving out while he cums. He kisses my neck, whispering sweet words to me as he starts to come down from his orgasm, telling me how good I am, how amazing I'm doing, how he could sit like this forever, buried deep inside of me, consuming me forever. I let his words soak in, letting them brand my soul, letting them claim me, because they do. His words claim me, taking a piece of me that I didn't know I wanted to give.

He fucks the rest of his cum inside of me, both of us a sweaty fucking mess by the end of it, and then he kisses me, his tongue saying so much, giving me all of the reassurance that I need, all of the confirmation that I'm secretly asking for. He pulls away, holding himself up with one arm, cupping my cheek with the other, and his eyes bore into mine, looking at me in a way I've never seen him look at anything.

He doesn't say anything, just stares at me for a second, before kissing me again, my entire body sinking into the kiss, desperate for more even though I'm exhausted, my body wrung out by him.

He sinks down next to me as he pulls out, scooping me into his arms so my back is against his front, his cock already hardening between us. We are a mess of sweaty limbs, but he doesn't seem to care, his entire body pressed against mine. We take a second to just breathe, a sense of peace coming over us, and I hate to admit it, but I enjoy being like this with him, being calm, content in his presence.

I stare at the window in front of us, the moonlight gleaming outside, the world still going around even though everything inside of this hotel room has changed. We aren't the same people that came in here, not even close, and it feels like when we leave, everything will be different too, like the world shifted.

"Our parents are going to freak out," I mutter, my voice quiet, the reality of this hitting me, and even though I'm ready for the fear, for the lack of trust in him, it doesn't come. As much as I want to push away from this, pretend there is nothing here, I know I can't. I know there is truth to his words, and I'm done pretending I don't feel it.

"They will probably be excited we are getting along for once," he says into my hair, his mouth already on my neck again, as if he can't get enough of me, can't last a minute without his lips against my skin. I stay silent, just thinking, enjoying the feeling of him against me, of him kissing me so softly that I can barely feel it as I sink into the exhaustion, finally letting it overtake me, my body completely relaxed, a sense of peace radiating through me.

He lifts his head and looks at me for a second, and I feel my eyes start to close, my body finally giving out, finally letting sleep take it.

"You aren't getting scared now, are you?" he whispers, his voice just barely vulnerable, as if he is actually worried I could walk away from this, as if he thinks that I have a chance of leaving him after the night we shared.

"No," I say matter-of-factly, albeit fuzzy from sleep, my eyes staying closed as I sink into slumber. "I'm not going anywhere," I mutter, and I know, I'm telling the truth, and that when we leave here, everything is going to be different. This Christmas isn't going to be like all the others, and although that scares me, makes me unsure of what to expect, I know we need to figure it out, because sometimes, things are too good to let fear get in the way.

Chapter Thirteen

Theo

We wake up slowly, both of us fucking exhausted, our alarms blaring for us to wake up, but I wait until the last second, needing to feel her against me, to feel her body pressed against mine so that I know last night was real.

It doesn't feel real. It feels like she is going to wake up and instantly glare at me, look at me with her gaze filled with disgust, like I'm the last person she wants to be stuck in this room with, the same way she looked at me last night when we entered.

But when her eyes finally open, her gaze still sleepy, her body probably sore from my heavy use of it last night, she smiles at me. It is still timid, like she doesn't know what to make of this yet, like she still has one foot out the door, but honestly, that's what I expected. I know I have a lot of ground to make up, a lot of groveling that needs to be done to show her how I truly feel about her, but I'm gonna fucking do it because I know she is worth it.

"Morning," I mutter against her ear, my voice low, my cock already stiff against her ass, wanting more from her, even though we did plenty last night. I don't know if it's ever going to be enough for me, if I'm ever going to be able to get enough from her because I'm always going to want another taste, another dip inside of her tight fucking cunt. I don't know how I'm going to survive now that she's mine. I might have to take a little vacation from school, just so I can soak her in, and really claim her the way that she deserves.

"Morning," she replies, snuggling back into the blankets, as if the last thing she wants to do is get up, and I feel my heart start to beat inside of my chest, excitement at watching her change the way she acts around me. She thinks she is discreet, I know she does, but I can see the peace on her face, the relaxation of her body. I can read her better than she can read herself because I've been doing it for fucking years, and I know she wants this, no matter how much it freaks her out.

I start kissing her neck, my lips moving on their own accord, my body primed and ready for her, desperate for another taste. Now that I've started, I'm not sure how I'm going to stop. She is too tempting, too enticing for me to resist, but I'm going to have to learn because we have Christmas with our families today, and I'm not sure how she is going to feel about telling them just yet.

I know she's scared, worried that this is all a sick joke, but I couldn't care less at this point. I'm here for the long haul, here to show her how desperately I've wanted her for so long, and I'm not going to let her fear stop me. I'm going to prove to her, prove to us, to the whole fucking world, that she has been mine from the start. I just neglected to tell her, to prove to her that I deserve her.

"What time is it?" she asks, her voice groggy, still thick with sleep, and I rub my cock against her ass, my body desperate for her, even though I know the answer to her question is going to push us out of bed. I know we need to get going because check out is in ten minutes, but I don't know if I'm going to be able to get out of this bed if she is still in it.

"Don't worry about that," I soothe, my lips against her throat, and she turns just slightly, giving me better access. I smile into her skin, her body already responding to me, already hungry for me, and slide my hand across her belly, so fucking slowly making my way down. The need to touch her, to feel her against me, to have my fingers inside of her, overwhelms me. It

127

consumes my every thought, her entire being taking over my soul, leaving me with nothing other than her. She consumes me, her body against mine. Everything is her her her now and I can't get enough.

She moans when my hand finally makes contact with her cunt, my fingers sliding against her clit, her pussy already wet for me. I groan into her neck, my cock literally straining to be inside of her, to feel all of this wetness that is just for me. I slide my other hand under her body, instantly cupping her tit in my hand, squeezing, pinching her nipple in between my fingers, my mind only on her.

She moans into my touch, her voice breathy, her body needy as she arches for me, urging me on.

"We need to get up, don't we?" she asks, but her body knows what it wants. Her hips thrust against my fingers, taking her own pleasure from me, her nipple hardening in my fingers, her chest arching up, asking for more, asking for me to keep going. I keep kissing her neck, keeping my mouth busy so I don't have to lie to her, while my hands continue making her moan, the sound urging me on while my cock leaks pre-cum against her ass.

I slide a finger inside of her, using the palm of my hand to rub against her clit, and she moans for me, so fucking loud, louder than she has yet, and I watch as her walls come down just a little more. I watch as she gives me another piece of herself, her insecurity in us dissolving another fraction, and my control snaps, the urge to make her cum, right here, right now, consuming my every thought, my body moving without my consent because I need her cum on my fingers. I need to feel her fall apart for me, giving herself to me.

Her hips thrust against my fingers, her body desperate for this, her body using my hand and I try not to cum on her ass, desperately try not to embarrass myself by cumming early, cumming before I've even had a chance to slip inside of her, inside of her warm heat, her tight cunt. I need to feel her wrapped around me while I cum, and unfortunately, this morning, we don't have time for that. But we do have time for her to cum at least, which might be able to sustain me until we get back home, and I can take my time with her again, unwrapping her as my present this Christmas.

"Fuck," she mutters as I slide another finger inside, fucking her with force, desperate to feel her wrap around me, while my hand palms her tit, loving the feel of her in my grasp, in my arms, loving the feeling of being inside of her.

I slip a third finger inside, needing to feel her stretch, and she moans for me, her moans consuming me, ripping pleasure from my body as if she is touching me, and I try like hell to hold on, because I can feel how close I am, how close I am to painting her ass in my cum, and I don't know if I'm going to be able to last when she clenches around my fingers.

"Baby," she mutters, so softly I barely hear it, her voice so timid when she says it, and it means something to me that she would call me such a sweet fucking name, as if she is starting to see what I see, feel what I feel. As if she is starting to feel this all-consuming need to be with me, once and for all, for us to just have our way with each other. I can't stay away any longer, not anymore.

"Cum for me," I mutter in her ear, groaning as I feel her orgasm start, her cunt squeezing my fingers, pulsing around me, and I grind my cock into her ass, desperate for anything I can get from her as she uses my hand, her body spasming now, her legs shaking, her moans bouncing off the walls, surrounding me.

She comes down slowly, and I do my best to wring out her pleasure, to get every ounce I can, to fuck her body more, to keep the pleasure going, and when she is finally sated, I pull out of her, regretfully so, and kiss her, bending her head toward me. I need her mouth on mine before we leave the room where we found each other.

I pull away just barely, my desire to stay in bed all day almost taking over, but I pull away, leaning over to look at the time, seeing that check out was three minutes ago, and we need to leave before the front desk calls us, something I'm not in the mood to deal with.

"We have to get up," I say sadly, kissing her neck, wanting her to ask me to stay in bed because honestly, I would. If she asked me to, I would stay here all day, making her cum over and over again until she couldn't take anymore, until her body was shutting down, sleep taking her under.

"Ugh," she groans, her body lifting, the blanket falling down as she sits up, her tits on full display in front of me, and I resist the urge to pull her back, to force her to stay, because we really do need to fucking leave, no matter how desperately I don't want to.

It doesn't take either of us long to get ready, both of us having nothing more to pack than the clothes on our back, her purse, and my wallet. It only takes a few minutes, but part of me wishes it would take longer, that we could sit in this room for another minute, just basking in it, just enjoying being here, being in the place where everything changed for us, but we have to get home, back to reality, and I can only hope that we can keep this thing between us, the thing we found here, this passion and chemistry and trust.

We make our way down to the front desk, both of us quiet, probably from exhaustion, neither of us getting enough sleep last night, but when I reach out to hold her hand, she smiles at me, a small smile, a timid smile, and I know instantly it's going to be okay. This is an adjustment for both of us, but honestly, she is mine whether she likes it or not. I'm not letting her go, not after this.

We reach the front desk, and I hand the keys to the receptionist sitting there, a kind-looking woman in her mid-twenties, with short blonde hair and heavy eye makeup. I don't say anything, even though I probably should, since the fucking power was out all night, but I'm too tired to care, too exhausted to complain right now.

She looks down at the keys, thanking me, and turning to her computer. I go to walk away, but she looks at the keys with a confused expression that makes me halt, and I wait for her to say something. She just stares at the computer, typing a few things, her eyebrows raising, as if she is starting to understand, and I stand there, trying to figure out what is going on.

"Everything okay?" I ask, my voice curious, my gut holding me in place, needing to know why she was looking at our key card like that.

"Oh yes, sorry," she mutters sheepishly, her eyes still on the computer. "You were in room two thirty-five?" she asks, her gaze finally reaching mine again, and she looks confused too.

I nod, not understanding what she means.

"Oh, I just didn't think anyone was put there. We were told to keep that side empty since we weren't booked much last night," she says, waving her hands as if it isn't that big of a deal, as if her words mean nothing, but they jar me, reality not making sense for a second.

"Wait, you weren't booked up last night?" Autumn chimes in next to me, her understanding hitting before mine. The receptionist looks between us as if she is trying to understand where our confusion is coming from.

"We had like ten rooms booked," she says, her voice cautious. "Why?" she asks, an awkward smile taking over her face. I turn toward Autumn, my lips thinning into a line as I try to calm myself down, try not to let my anger overtake me, because this isn't the nice receptionist's fault. This is Cam's fault, and I could ruin his whole fucking life.

"The man working last night told us that you were fully booked. Only one room left," I mutter, my voice hard as I try to calm down.

"Oh," she says, still not quite understanding. "I'm not sure why he would tell you that. We only booked about a tenth of the hotel last night. And I thought the circuit was out on that whole side of the hotel," she mutters as if she is still trying to figure out the problem, but for me, everything clicks into place.

"That fucking bastard," I mutter under my breath, finally understanding his scheme. He thinks he's fucking smart, putting the both of us together, and turning the power off on us, leaving us to fucking freeze in that room.

"Do I need to call my manager?" the receptionist looks between the both of us, a glint of worry in her gaze as she tries to assess the situation.

I know what he was trying to do, trying to set the two of us up for this, so we would be forced together. I drunkenly told him once, about my feelings, and he thinks he's so fucking smart for this, like he is a little goddamn matchmaker, but he killed the heat to our room in a fucking snowstorm. We could have fucking frozen to death. *Autumn* could have frozen to death.

I feel my body fill with anger, the idea of her not being okay, being hurt, making my blood fucking boil.

But right when I start to nod my head, evil intentions filling my body, I feel Autumn put her hand on my arm, the touch instantly soothing me, and I glance over at her, and her eyes are soft, timid, and she stares at me, a small pleading in her gaze, as if she wants me to let this go, to resist my anger, and suddenly I think about what this would mean if I blew off the handle right now.

I don't regret anything that happened. I don't regret going into that room, holding her body down, and forcing her to cum, for fucking her. I don't even regret the accident. I hate that she has been put in danger far too many times over the last twenty-four hours, but I don't regret a single thing because it put us here, in each other's arms, leaving this hotel together, intent on seeing things through.

I can't regret that, I never could.

And if I freak out right now, if I let my anger take over, she might think that I do. Her fear might take her over, her uncertainty in our relationship might consume her, and I know at this moment, I can't give her any reason to doubt me, any reason to think that I'm not all in, that I'm not going to beg and plead with her to make this work.

I glance back at the receptionist, who is still looking at me, waiting for my answer, and I take a deep breath, my body calming as I remind myself that it worked out, that even if I hate what Cam did, his plan worked. I'm walking out of here with everything I have ever wanted, and unfortunately, I have him to thank for it.

I'm still going to punch him in the face the next time I see him.

"No," I finally reply with a small nod, the air thick around us as the tension peaks. I glance at Autumn, and a small smile curves her lips as her eyes bore into mine. She tries to hide it, tries to pretend that my reaction didn't just calm her, but I know her too well to let that pass. "It's all fine," I say with a tight smile, and I turn away, desperate to leave this place once and for all, to leave this place with the only thing I've ever wanted anyway.

Epilogue

Autumn

"Oh my god, this place is so romantic," my mom says, gushing, glancing around the lobby, her eyes taking everything in as if we are at a national park, at a seventh wonder of the world, but instead we are in a decent hotel at the edge of the road where we crashed the car last year, and she is in awe of their neutral decorations and the too nice smell that we all know is synthetic.

I push away my annoyance, glancing over at Theo, using his body, his gaze, to calm myself down. Our moms insisted on coming here again, on making it a new yearly tradition, adding to all of the others, and I hate to take this away from them, hate to spoil their fun.

"Oh my god, can we remake that night?" Carol asks, my mom instantly looking at her with her jaw dropped, rushing into a chorus of "yes"s, both of them squealing in the corner as we approach the front desk. Theo and I pretend that we don't know them. I may be annoyed, may feel a little embarrassed about this whole thing, like it is taking the night my life changed, taking the night I won't soon forget, and making it a show, but I feel myself grin, enjoying the way Theo takes my hand as he approaches the desk, a grin on his face, a smirk, as if he likes being back, likes being here again.

"We have two reservations," Theo says beside me, our moms following close behind, their voices radiating around the lobby. He talks to the receptionist, one who hopefully isn't going to cut power to our room all night, and gets our room keys, the same room we stayed in last year, and the one right next to it for our moms.

"Do you host weddings here?" my mom interrupts, right when we are about to leave, and I feel my face redden, the vulnerability of the question making my insides squeeze together.

"Mom," I mutter, desperate for her to cut it out, but she just ignores me, waiting for the receptionist to answer.

"Not really, the lobby is a bit too small for that," the woman behind the desk answers softly, looking a little uncomfortable at the question, her eyes darting around our group, trying to figure out the correct response.

We walk away, my mom probably still planning a wedding in her mind, even though the place is too fucking small, thinking about where the flowers would look best around the lobby, and what time of year would be best for this part of the country, and I feel myself sink into Theo, just barely, our shoulders touching, using his body to physically comfort me.

It's not that I'm uncomfortable with weddings. I'm just a little uncomfortable that my wedding could be here. Theo has been slow with me, giving me time, giving me enough trust for the both of us, but big steps, like I love yous and things like that, are still hard for me.

He is patient, and he is sweet, giving me all the space I need, fucking me whenever I get an ounce of fear, and he hasn't pushed me. He has worked for my trust, treating me kindly every step of the way, and after a while, it just felt nice to be with him without the push to talk about the future, without the pressure to talk about what this would become, what feelings are between us.

But the longer this goes on, the more I want him to know, that I see that future with him, that I want everything he has wanted, that the feelings he confessed to me in this very hotel, are mutual, that I feel them too, that they consume me, but I'm not sure how to bring it up, how to broach the subject, and it's been easier to avoid it than to say anything.

So my mom bringing it up, when I haven't even had the courage to, makes me sweat.

"I'm just imagining you guys passing all of this, but instead of holding hands, you were probably glaring at each other," Carol mutters, looking around as the elevator doors open to a hallway. My mom is giddy next to her, both of them huddled together, glancing around like this isn't the exact same layout of every hotel in the world.

I roll my eyes, trying to be discreet, but my mom sees, and she gives me a glare.

"I'm just trying to experience the place where you fell in love, Autumn," she says like I'm ruining her fun. Usually, when she makes a comment about us being in love, I brush it off, claiming that we didn't fall in love in this hotel, we just fell into each other and realized what we could be, but it doesn't feel quite right to push it away anymore, to pretend that what I feel for him is anything less than complete and utter love, complete and utter devotion.

I want him all the time, want to be near him, want his body pressed against mine, his lips on my neck. I've never felt like this before, so overwhelmed by emotion, by pure need, that it consumes my thoughts throughout the day. I've never been so attached to someone, and it used to scare me, used to make me fearful of what would happen, but the longer we have stayed together, the longer he has shown me the exact man that he is, the more my fear has died away.

We finally walk to our rooms, and our moms rush in the second we put the key card in, glancing around the small space, squealing with each other. I think we are more here for them than for us. I'm sure they could have done this without us, staying in the room themselves, but they wouldn't let us off the hook that easily.

"Okay, mom, can you be done now?" I ask, hating the attention on us. I know our moms are happy for us, but it doesn't make it any more awkward to have your mom walk into the room you first fucked your boyfriend, both of you knowing it.

"Okay, okay, we will go check out our room," she says, finally giving in to my pleas. She walks toward me, taking my head in her hands, giving my forehead a kiss, before patting Theo on the cheek. Carol follows with the same, before leaving the room, the door clicking behind them. The quiet suddenly feels weird without their energy to fill it.

Theo looks at me, and his gaze feels heavy, like it means something, and I stare back, my body fucking tuned into him, tuned into this room. It feels weird being back, weird seeing it again, exactly like I remember, but a little different, too. It has been long enough that my mind has started to fill in some of the blanks, some of the pieces I don't remember, and now they are surrounding me, looking different than my brain assumed.

"Come here," Theo mutters, his voice a low rumble, and I react to it, knowing exactly what it means, knowing what his body wants even just from the sound of his voice alone. I walk toward him, slowly, my attention drawn to him so fucking quickly. He comforts me, taking every ounce of fear, every ounce of discomfort out of me, ridding it all from my body. I soak it up, remembering not long ago when it wasn't like this, when his presence didn't bring such peace, but I don't think about that for long.

I lean into him, his arms coming around me, and we just stand like that for a second, lightly hearing our moms in the room next door, and after a few minutes, when I'm feeling better, more centered, we walk over to their room, leaving our stuff in ours, leaving the unpacking for later.

We spend the night in the lobby, playing games with our parents, our dads and Theo's siblings coming just for a few hours, leaving our moms to have the room to themselves for a girl's night. We just have fun, absorbing the space, and I feel myself lean into Theo more than normal, the feel of his body bringing me peace, bringing me a sense of calm, just being around him being too fucking much for me.

It finally hits late enough that all of us are tired, our energy slowly fading, and we say goodbye to our dads and Kylie and Griffin, all of them leaving early, knowing tomorrow is just going to be a bigger day of festivities, and we start to head upstairs with our moms.

The elevator doors open to the second floor and we step out, a little buzzed off cheap ass wine, holiday music playing overhead, laughing lightly at something stupid my mom said, a joke that has been going on all night, and wasn't even funny at first, but the more someone says it, the funnier it gets.

I feel happy, in a way I didn't expect to, in a way I've never experienced. I'm surrounded by all of my favorite people at Christmas time, all of them enveloping me in their happiness, and I feel comforted, safe.

We say goodbye to our moms, both of them looking exhausted since they stayed up so late, and walk into our room, the room that only a year ago was a prison, leaving the lights off as we enter, as if we already know our way around the space, as if we are more comfortable here without any light, because that's how we know this place.

Theo looks at me, the moonlight the one way I can make out the shapes of his face, and he looks at me with so much meaning. This night isn't just another Christmas Eve. This is big. This marks a year of us being together, of us trusting each other, of leaning into this thing between us. He walks toward me, slowly, so fucking slowly that I feel like I might burst if he doesn't touch me, doesn't stop looking at me with so much goddamn love that it makes it hard to breathe.

He kisses me, his lips pressing down on mine softly, so fucking soft at first, both of us just exploring, feeling each other as if for the first time. I feel my stomach swirl, thinking about our first night here, how new it all felt, how scary, and although I feel that too, this year, I'm too overwhelmed with love, with comfortability, with a sense of pure desire, even more than lust, to feel anxious.

"This room makes me fucking horny," Theo whispers, his crass words conflicting with the tone of the night. I smile as he pulls away, leaving our foreheads connected. He places his hands on my hips, his fingers digging into me. I lean into him, pressing my body against him, desperate for more.

"You're ridiculous," I mutter with a smile, not even thinking before I speak, desperately wanting him to kiss me again, to claim me in this room just like he did last year, to make me feel everything I felt, every emotion, every fear, every ounce of pleasure. I want it all. I want to be reminded of what was found here, of what we discovered, and I want to feel it again every year, reminding myself that there was always more than I thought between us, that it was just a waiting game until we became more.

"Autumn," he mutters, bringing my chin up to look at him, our eyes connecting in the dark room. "I'm gonna fuck you on that bed, just like I did last year, and you're going to take it, like a good fucking girl, aren't you?" he asks, his voice light, but his words have an edge to them, as if he wants me to fight back, as if he wants me to go against him, to pick a fight.

But if there is anything I've learned since fucking him that first night, since finding my way to him, it's that some fights, aren't worth picking, and this is one I'm not going to even try because I want this just as badly as he wants to give it. I don't want to fight with him, not tonight.

No, tonight, I want to commit to him, want to show him all the emotions I've been hiding away, all the feelings I have been too scared to say. I want to use my body to say all the things

I'm too scared to vocalize because I'm not sure if I'm strong enough yet to say it, but he needs to know how I feel.

"You can't last one night without fucking me?" I ask, my voice coy, a small smile taking over my face, and I watch as his eyes darken as I challenge him, not resisting him, just giving me a hard time.

"No," he says simply before pushing me onto the bed. I don't even know it's happening until I huff a breath with my back against the comforter, shock radiating through me. He climbs over me, his body instantly molding to mine, as if he has been like this a hundred times, as if he knows exactly where he needs to touch to make me desperate for him.

His hands are all over me, needy and desperate, taking hold of my hips, locking me into place. I glance at him, my eyes wide, and he just grins, enjoying having me exactly where he wants me, where he needs me. One of his hands leaves my hip, trailing up my stomach, in between my tits, so fucking slowly, so careful not to touch exactly where I want him to, and right when I think he is going to stop, when I think he is finally going to touch me, he trails up higher, until his hand is around my throat, squeezing, just enough for me to feel the pressure, for me to feel his possession over me. "You're not going to leave this bed until I'm done with you, got it?" he says, his voice so fucking dominating, so fucking commanding. I feel my desire roll through me, my entire body craving this, craving him to take control, just like that first fucking night, while he held me down and used my body for his own desires.

I stare into his eyes, submitting to him without words. I hear the sound before I register the pain, a small slap radiating off the walls, my cheek feeling the sharp pain of a slap. His hand only left my throat for a second, before returning, adding more pressure to the sides of my throat, cutting off my blood supply. "Answer me, Autumn," he says, his voice hard, but his eyes are so fucking soft, as if he is asking me for permission, asking me for consent in the only way he knows how.

"Okay," I mutter, his fingers squeezing against my throat, and I writhe against him, my entire body so fucking horny, my every goddamn nerve ending at his disposal. I want this, so desperately. I want to get lost in him, want him to get lost in me, want to resurface hours later remembering that the world is still spinning while we are stuck in our own little world.

"I bet you're already fucking wet for me, aren't you?" he asks, using his hand on my throat to turn my gaze to his, locking our eyes together.

I nod, his hand around my throat making it hard to speak, but I wouldn't trust my voice anyway. He smiles at my movement, a devilish smile, like it overjoys him to know how much he affects me, how horny I am for him, how he knows every kinky thing I want him to do, how I want him to take all of the control.

"I'm going to sink inside of that tight pussy, and you're just going lay there and take my cock, aren't you?" he asks, his voice so fucking close to my ear, I can feel his breath against my skin, and it sends shivers down my spine. My entire body is so desperate for it, for him to fuck me, for him to control me.

I used to hate this, the feeling of him taking over, of him forcing me, telling me what to do. I hated it and loved it at the exact same time. Loved how it made me feel, hated giving him the power. But the longer we are together, the more I've grown used to it, craved his power, craved him to take all of the decisions away from me, to just let me sink into the pleasure.

"Stroke my cock," he whispers, his lips pressing against the shell of my ear, his teeth scraping against the skin, and I inhale a breath. I bring my hand down, finding its way inside of his pants, then boxers, desperate for a feel. I don't pull him out yet, leaving his pants in between us while my hand explores him through his jeans. I stroke him, once, twice. He groans into my ear, the sound bouncing around in my head, consuming my every thought. I feel my body respond to him, to his moans while I thrust his cock into my hand, knowing that as much as he likes showing me who is in control, I have just as much power as he does. He is desperate for me, has been for so fucking long. He kisses the ground I walk on, desperate for an ounce of my time, an ounce of my attention. He worships my body, coaxing pleasure from me, but when we are like this, in bed together, this dynamic is my favorite, him telling me what to do, and me listening like a good little slut.

"God, your hand feels so fucking good," he says in between his groans. His hips thrust into my hand, forcing me to take him all the way to the base of his cock. He's all around me, his body pressed against mine, his cock in my hand, his breath against my neck, his moans in my ear, and it's completely overwhelming in the best way.

"Please fuck me," I beg, desperate for him to finally put me out of misery, for him to take what he owns, what he has owned for so long. I haven't been able to tell him, haven't known how to express what I'm feeling, to explain the way he makes me feel when I've been so used to the hate between us, but it's fucking true. This man owns me, just like I've owned him for longer than I've even known. He owns my body, my mind, my fucking soul, and I want to show him, want to let him have my body right now, want to give myself to him so that he can understand all of the crazy and wild emotions storming through my fucking head.

"Oh, you want me to fuck you?" he asks, his voice so fucking condescending, as if he has me exactly where he wants me, as if this was his plan all along. I nod against his hand, desperate for this, not even fucking caring if I need to put my dignity on the floor, because with him, I'm too keyed up, too antsy for this. I can't hold myself back, not anymore. "Wouldn't that be so awful, if I just made you jerk me off, and then I left you to fucking wait?" he asks, and I feel my defiance spark, the strong-willed part of me desperate to tell him off, to show him how I know that I own him too, that we are equals in this, but I want to show him how committed I am to him, how badly I want this, so I hold back, giving him all of the power, giving him the control, knowing I could take it for myself but choosing not to.

"Please," I whimper, and I feel his cock twitch in my hand as I speak, my fucking voice egging his body on, pushing him closer and closer to orgasm, and that thought sends lust shooting through me, watching him become consumed by me, become obsessed with me, does things to my body that I can't even describe.

"You're going to have to be quiet if I fuck you," he says, his voice holding a warning, the earlier slap flashing back into my mind, and although that is supposed to deter me, part of me wants to be loud, to make him punish me, to make him slap me until my cheek is fucking red, until there is physical evidence to what we have, of the chemistry between us.

"I promise, I can be quiet," I whisper, my voice a fucking quiver, desperation leaking from my every goddamn pore. It would be embarrassing if I didn't know he felt the same.

He moves me quickly, rolling me onto my stomach with barely any effort, moving my body for his own pleasure. I lift my hips instantly, impatient. I'm desperate for him to take my clothes off, to see how wet I actually am.

"God, you're a fucking horny thing tonight, aren't you?" he asks, his voice in my ear, his body hovering over mine, his cock pressed in between my ass cheeks. Even through my leggings and his jeans, I can feel how hard he is, how badly he wants me. I can feel the heat of him, his desire just as obvious as my own. "Why is that?" he mutters, grinding against me, groaning into me. "Hm?" he asks again when I don't answer and I try to focus on his words, his body consuming my every thought.

"I don't know," I mutter, and I feel his body lift just enough for him to smack my ass, my left ass cheek stinging with the sensation, and a moan leaks out of my mouth before I can stop it. I clutch the sheet beneath me, my body too sensitive for this.

"Yes, you do," he replies, running his hand up my ass, kneading it with his fingers, soothing the ache.

"No, I don't," I reply, a little defiance in my tone, but we both know I'm lying, both know there is something more to today for both of us, some more meaning than there usually is.

"I'm not going to fuck you until you say it, Autumn," he mutters in my ear, biting my ear lobe, driving me fucking insane, my heart skipping a beat inside of my chest, and I let out sigh, lifting my ass to grind against him, trying to take what I want, trying to use his body for my pleasure, but he just laughs lightly. "You can get yourself close, baby, but I'm not going to let you cum until you say it," he says, his voice thick with emotion, with a need for me to confess what today means to me. I've been the one holding back, the one with one foot out the door, the fear always in the back of my mind, something I haven't been able to shake, and I know he needs this from me, needs me to finally commit to this, to finally let go of all the bullshit that used to be there.

"I'm thinking about last year," I finally mutter, my voice so fucking low, and I talk into the pillow, trying desperately to muffle the sound. I'm glad he is not facing me, not looking me in the eyes, which now that I think about it, is probably something he did on purpose, trying to give me the courage to say this, to expose myself in front of him.

"What are you thinking about," he asks, his voice light, and it has a calming effect on me, just his fucking voice making me feel safer, making me feel like I can do this, can finally get this out of the way, tell him how I've been feeling without worrying about what is going to happen between us.

"How..." My voice gives out on me, my fear squeezing at my throat, but I push through, knowing I need to, knowing that I want more from us than this, than this half-in-half-out bullshit. "How good it felt to finally be together, to be with you," I whisper, grinding into him, needing to move my body, needing him to reassure me, in the best fucking way he knows how, in the way that has worked for so long, that has made me feel seen and loved by him.

Loved. That's how it makes me feel, to fuck him, to feel his body against mine, like he loves me, and I know he fucking does.

"Lift your hips," he says, as if it is a reward, and truthfully, it feels like it is. It feels like he is rewarding me for telling him, for exposing myself, and I feel that work through me, relief that he is finally going to end this, to fuck me like I need him to.

I do what he asks, lifting my hips for him, and he rests his knees on each side of my legs, and he pulls my leggings and underwear down, just enough for him to fuck me, as if he can't imagine wasting another second without being inside of me.

"Another time, I'll take my time, make you fucking beg for it," he says, his body still moving just barely, and I know without even looking that he is taking his cock out, the zipper of his pants ringing through the room. I press my legs together, anticipation driving me wild. "But this time, I can't fucking wait. I need to be inside of you," he says, his voice a fucking breath. I feel his hands spread my ass apart, giving him access to me. I separate my legs as best I can, arching up for him, and feel the tip of his cock right against my cunt, and I literally whimper, so desperate, so fucking needy for him to fuck me I actually don't know if I can breathe without it, if I can exist another second without him inside of me. I'm an addict, my next fix right there, so close I can almost taste it, and I'm craving it so badly, I would do anything for it.

He slides the first inch in, and I sigh with fucking relief, pleasure wrapping around me, and when he moves to slide in another inch, I let out a strangled cry before I can think twice, my body just responding to him.

"I thought I told you to be quiet?" he asks, giving me no warning, before sliding his full length inside of me, a punishing stroke, giving me no time to adjust, just forcing me to stretch around him like I have a thousand other times. I hold back my moan this time, moaning into my pillow as my cunt pulses around him, already so fucking close to cumming, already right on the edge, and he knows it. He pushed me for too long, and now I'm so close, my body primed for him.

"I'm trying," I mutter into the pillow, as he starts fucking me, his thrusts hard and fast, giving me everything he has, fucking me with all of his power. I do my best not to moan with each thrust, my body already starting to spasm, my legs shaking under him. I feel right on the edge, my orgasm so fucking close, within reach, and I want to tip over, want that bliss more than I want to breathe.

"Don't you dare fucking cum yet," he mutters, fucking me hard enough that our skin slaps together, but he muffles the sound by stopping just barely before the crack of our bodies, not wanting the whole hotel to hear us fuck, but I can still make out the sound, the way his hips are thrusting into me with force, and I try like fucking hell, to push my orgasm away, but it's so hard when he's fucking me like this.

"I c-can't," I whimper out, barely hanging on. "I'm gonna fucking cum," I moan, not knowing if I can hold it back, not when he's giving it to me this fucking good.

He leans forward, holding himself up with one hand, his other angling around my head, cupping my jaw, his hips still fucking into me, his cock hitting me deeper, thrusting hard, and my eyes start to roll to the back of my head, my entire body consumed with the pleasure that he is giving me, not allowing me to focus on anything else.

"Don't fucking cum," he spits out, his teeth clenched, but I feel him pulsing inside of me, feeling his arm shaking as he tries to hold himself up while fucking me, pleasure wrapping around him too, making it hard to think about anything other than each other, anything other than the way that this between us, this chemistry, this thing, is all consuming. "Until I tell you that you can," he finished, his voice breathy, as if he is barely hanging on, but his threat hangs in the air, and I try to breathe, try not to focus on the pleasure, on the desire thrumming between my legs, but it is so hard.

He lifts back up, fucking into me, groaning lightly, just loud enough for me to hear, and something about it feels so fucking intimate, that we can share this together, that we are the only ones who see this side of each other. I feel so connected to him, so overpowered by my want, my need to be with him, to be around him constantly. He feels like this missing part of me that I tried to push away for so long, and I'm finally, fucking finally, embracing it.

"Fuck. I'm going to cum soon, and when I do, you're going to cum with me," he mutters, his voice low. I pull myself back off the edge again, just barely, my body literally so close at every second. Even his voice could push me, a mere touch, a breath of fucking air, right over the edge and into straight bliss.

I moan, loudly, not covering it up, not having the thought to do so, and he leans back over my body, his hand cupping over my mouth, and I feel my eyes roll back, his entire body consuming me in this moment, all around me at once, and it's too much. I can't take it, can't keep myself from cumming, from giving my all into this.

"Holy fuck, you're so fucking tight baby," he says, and I know he's right there with me, right on the edge. I groan into his hand, his fingers catching some of the sound, and I get lost in the sensations of his cock inside of me, completely fucking filling me. "I'm gonna fucking cum inside of you," he groans, before his mouth is on my shoulder, and he is biting into my skin, my body catching all of his sounds, and I fall right off with him, my entire world exploding all at once, all in one moment, as I have one of the best orgasms of my life.

His body falls right next to me as we both start to come down, his side pressed against mine, keeping us connected. He kisses my shoulder, kisses the bite mark he left, his hands trailing up and down my back, his fingertips just barely pressed into my skin, his touch calming me in more ways than he will ever understand.

It's slow, the way we find our way back into each other's arms, me turning just barely and him scooping me up, both of us needing more contact, not done with each other yet. I lay against his chest, his arm around me, cupping me to him, pressing me tight, as if he never wants to let go. I feel my pulse slow, my entire body relaxing against him, loving the feel of him like this, in this room once again.

He plays with my hair, his fingers caressing me with some-thing so close to love, it fills me with warmth, and I feel the words on the tip of my tongue, anxiety spilling in my gut, but he speaks first, his deep voice radiating around the room, the walls knowing our story better than we do.

"You didn't correct your mom this time," he whispers, his voice low, the tiniest hint of fear deep in there. I stare at the ceiling and think about what he said, trying to make sense of his words in my orgasm-hazy brain.

"What do you mean?" I ask, not getting it.

"She said this is the place that we fell in love, and whenever she says that, you'd correct her, telling her that we aren't in love," he says, his hands still in my hair, as if to be a physical reminder that he isn't going anywhere, that he is still here, and he intends to be throughout everything.

"Yeah?" I reply, wanting him to talk more, the confession I just had on the tip of my tongue suddenly feels so big, so scary, and now I'm not sure if I'm ready to say it.

"I just want you to know, even if you don't say it back," he says, pausing, leaving me on edge, waiting for his next words, my heartbeat in my ears. "I've loved you since before that night, and I didn't want to tell you and scare you, but I have felt it for so fucking long," he confesses. It feels like the air is sucked out of the room, a good sensation and bad at the same time. My heart is full, hearing him confess this, hearing that it has been so long for him, that I've never had any reason to fear. But it's also tough because I know what I need to do now. I need to finally be brave and take the leap to trust him fully, give into this relationship, and stop pretending that we aren't meant to be. Stop pretending that I don't want a cute wedding here, in this tiny ass hotel, in the place we fell in fucking love. I want it all, and I've been so full of fear, so reserved, that I haven't been able to see it, but I'm ready to face the truth because at least I know I will have him by my side.

"I love you too," I say, a whisper, just loud enough for both of us to hear, and then silence. The room feels too big, as I wait for his reaction, but even as a few beats pass, I don't feel that scared. I don't feel worried that he's going to brush me off because, for the past year, he has done nothing but show me how much he adores me, how much he loves me. I know I can rely on that.

He turns my body, so that I'm on my back, and he looks into my eyes, the room so dark that I can barely see him, but I would know this look even if I was blind, because he looks at me like this constantly, with adoration and love in his gaze. He doesn't speak, probably knowing that it's too big of a moment for me, instead, he kisses me, consuming my mouth with his, and we sink deeper into the bed, into the room where we fell in love, where we found each other, and where we continue to commit to each other.

Books By This Author

Done Right (She Teaches Him #1):

What happens when Emma, who just wants to be done right, meets Finn, who doesn't know what he's doing?

Taught Right (She Teaches Him #2):

What happens when Joey, who just wants to be taught right, hires Ava, who knows exactly how to teach him?

F*cked Right (She Teaches Him #3):

What happens when Jace, who has never done this before, gets f*cked right by Callie, who knows exactly what she's doing?

Greedy:

What happens when the best kind of revenge, is fucking your ex-boyfriend's business rival?

About This Author

Rhianna Burwell is an Amazon best seller in erotica. Author of the Before series and the She Teaches Him series, available on Kindle Unlimited, she takes pride in writing spicy, realistic, and deeply satisfying romance and erotica. Rhianna currently resides in Minnesota, where—when she's not writing erotica hot enough to melt all the winter snows—she enjoys curling up with her cat, avidly watching Grey's Anatomy, and reading—her current fav is alien romance. Rhianna loves to hear from readers, who can connect with via any of her social media links.

Instagram: @rhiannaburwellauthor

Tiktok: @rhiannaburwellauthor